T0375609

# AN IMPERFECT FAITH

*Rachel Malorie Taylor*

WestBow Press books may be ordered through booksellers or by contacting:

WestBow Press
A Division of Thomas Nelson & Zondervan
1663 Liberty Drive
Bloomington, IN 47403
www.westbowpress.com
844-714-3454



ISBN: 979-8-3850-2629-6 (sc)
ISBN: 979-8-3850-2631-9 (hc)
ISBN: 979-8-3850-2630-2 (e)

Library of Congress Control Number: 2024910722

Print information available on the last page.

WestBow Press rev. date: 07/29/2024

This book is dedicated to all my friends and family, my nursing colleagues, and to the Holy Spirit for giving me the vision and the courage to tell this story.

# CONTENTS

# CHAPTER 1

He stared down at a blank sheet of paper, rubbing his furrowed forehead, trying to conjure up words like a genie from a magic lamp. He wasn't known for being a man of many words. Well, he had put it off long enough. Time to get it done. You'd think for a dollar help wanted ad it would actually include someone to help write it. He had to admit to himself, Serita was probably right. Writing this thing was her idea. She usually took care of writing letters for him or for that matter anything that required more than a quick note. Most he would do is add his signature as needed. Serita made sure he read everything first. Then after all the corrections he'd take the finished correspondence and mail them at the postmaster's office in Nightshade. Not that there were many letters to send. Over the years he relied on Serita to organize everything from legal papers to property or livestock documents. She insisted that he do his own writing for this situation though. Yep, Serita had saved him a lot of headaches when it came to paperwork.

But Sam was alone now. Left to the goings on of his own life.

His housekeeper, Serita Dalton, had left the ranch going on a month now. When her husband Tom died from consumption over a year ago. Serita had stayed to continue on as Sam's housekeeper. At this moment she was surely already settled following a two-day train trip out of Nightshade to Kansas City. Serita's sister had sent for her when she learned of Tom's death. Her sister, a widow herself, was having a hard time of it, so Serita packed up and made her way back to Kansas, back to her own family. She had been Sam's housekeeper for over fifteen years and was being called on to help out with her own family now. Sam depended on her and Tom to help him keep the ranch organized. And what a cook, Serita was the best cook in the county. Tom used to tell her that if she cooked dirt he would ask for seconds. Sam vouched for it. The ranch house was always clean and neat just as Sam preferred it. It was a comfort to him. His home. Serita and Tom were responsible for making it his home.

He rarely had to ask for anything. When he couldn't find his pocket watch, she knew where he left it. If she noticed the holes in his socks, she darned them. When the kerosene was getting low in the house lamps, she filled them, usually without him even knowing it needed doing. The accounting books and the financial records were all in place. Yes, everything was taken care of. It left Sam free to handle all the other details of the ranch. He didn't need a woman. Serita was all he needed to keep things running. Tom too, him being the right-hand man. Both of them were the reasons he had peace of mind. There were other important things for Sam to think about. The ranch required his daily attention. The Triple S was his woman. And that was enough women in his life.

# CHAPTER 2

Serita and her husband, Tom, lived in the house a young Sam had built for his intended, Amelia. It was a smaller house, smaller than the main house that he was born in, but it was perfect for a family starting out. While Serita was living in it with her two sons and Tom, there were some minor changes. Tom painted the outside a few times over the years. And later, he built onto the porch turning it into a wrap around with a red cedar swing. The main bedroom was modest but spacy. The boys each had a room of their own and there were several large windows throughout the house, which had been the only thing Amelia had wanted Sam to add. It was quite the home and Sam was proud of it then. He hammered the final nail just two days before the wedding. The day that Amelia stopped everything, him, their future, his life, and dreams.

Sam met her in town that day to tell her the good news about finishing the house. The wedding was to be held in the front yard of their new home. Most of the townsfolk were invited and were expected to attend.

Sam thought differently about Nightshade people then. They were friendly enough. He remembered them growing up. He watched his father and mother interact with them when they were in town on business. Then he was just a skinny six-year-old following his mother, hand in hand as she gathered up supplies while his father went ahead to the stockyards to check the livestock prices. She often stopped along the way to engage in small talk with the ladies that passed them. The lazy conversations about their day to day lives, sharing family news and stories was less than interesting to him. But to his mother it seemed to be more so. Most of the women just patted him on the head and told him how big he was getting as they sauntered off waiting for the next victim to come along. His mother usually stopped in at the post office to send letters off to distant family members full of the latest details about life on the Triple S. She finished shopping in the general store and collected her quilting samples and sometimes a few odds and ends furnishings. Then, they would load up in the buckboard with all the packages and parcels, leaving little room for the three of them to sit for the trip home. The ride included talk about the activities of the day and conversations of latest news out of Washington. Sam couldn't keep his eyes open and more times than not, drifted off to sleep halfway home. He looked forward to those trips. The memories. Later, as he grew, going to town meant spending less time with his mother and more and more time at the stockyards with his father. It was a proud day when at sixteen, Sam's father gave him his own Colt pistols to wear into town on the cattle drives to Nightshade. Such a different time then. So many changes in a lifetime.

Amelia was fond of Nightshade town life. She hadn't lived outside of it since birth. The ranch was a new world to her far from the hub of humanity. She met him on one of his trips to town. He was bringing cattle in with his father and the ranch hands one day late in the spring of that year. Sam was a strapping young man then. Six foot four, two hundred pounds of lean muscle and grit. On that bright crisp day riding into town, he saw her walking down the wood sidewalks of Nightshade. She stopped in front of one of the dress shops and was looking through the window. He took one look at her blue bonnet, pulled around her shiny brown hair and he couldn't stop staring. She saw him looking intently at her and she smiled at him. He spent the rest of the day with her instead of the stockyards. If it hadn't been for his father finding him, he would have missed going back to the ranch alone. He rode back to the Triple S a changed man. That was all. He was never the same.

Over summer and fall Sam made the trip back to town many

times. Each time it was harder than the last for him to leave. He remembered their first kiss. It was six months to the day when he saw her standing at the store window of Nightshade Dress and Petticoat.

That was when she said she loved him. It was the best day of his life. The second-best day was the day she agreed to marry him. Sam was looking forward to living life together. His parents were happy for them. They met Amelia and her parents after the date was set. Amelia's parents were amiable but a little too stiff in Sam's mind. He chalked it up to her being their only child. They were city folk to the core. They refused to allow her to visit the Triple S until the day of the wedding, but he was welcome to visit her with a chaperone. In other words, her father was within eyesight of them both. Sam, although disappointed, understood. After all her parents were respectable people; Sam didn't want to do anything to disparage Amelia's character or get off on the wrong foot with her or them. So, a few times a month, he made the trip to Nightshade and continued his courting of the fair Amelia.

Sam and his father built the honeymoon house the following spring on Triple S land. Sam enjoyed the time he spent with this father over the months putting up walls and raising the roof. He often discussed the process with Amelia. He didn't think Amelia was too concerned about the house. Hadn't even questioned it. She said she was looking forward to seeing it when it was finished. She asked about it occasionally. He hadn't been to town much since starting the house, but when he was able to, he stopped in to visit Amelia. Sam wanted everything to be perfect. She hadn't offered much about her ideas for the house. He'd asked her what she wanted for the kitchen and what color she wanted the walls to be or if she preferred a porch. Amelia just said do what he thought was best other than she preferred a lot of windows, but she left it to him to make those decisions. He tried to build it the way he thought she would like. A root and spring cellar were added to the property for food storage. Both of those were useful at the main house as well. As he thought back over it, he might have missed her meaning, when she mentioned that the old Palmer house was up for sale, and wouldn't it be a nice house for someone? At the time it had just seemed like a passing thought of conversation. But Sam was thinking that was something that her father might have told her. Surely, she hadn't expected him to leave the Triple S and move to town. He fooled himself. That was what she meant and sayin' so now just two days before the wedding. He couldn't understand it. Sam had asked her if she still loved him. But she didn't answer. Wouldn't even look in his eyes. She just offered up some thin apology telling him she wanted to be more than a plain simple ranch wife. And with that she turned, walked away, leaving him standing there in his boots, cold and confused. Maybe he hadn't spent enough time with her. He had been involved with building their home. Maybe he had neglected her too much. He just never could figure out the answers to those questions.

# CHAPTER 3

Amelia's parents didn't seem surprised about the canceled wedding. She was brought up to be a cultured woman, proud in the tradition of the finer things in life. Sam loved that about her. They were a blended mix of city girl, country boy that should have made one of those left-handed marriages. His parents liked the idea of having their son and new daughter-in-law living close by. Amelia was a true lady, well-bred in manners and carriage. Sam was thankful for it. Until Amelia, he thought he knew what love was.

But on that day, he only knew, love was painful.

After Amelia, somehow, he just couldn't seem to find the time to tear the new house down. And up until Tom and Serita moved in, he never set foot in it again. Truth be told, he still held onto the idea Amelia would change her mind. Though he'd never say it out loud. Eventually he was resigned to the truth that he couldn't tear it down. The house was all that was left, built out of love and happiness A visible sign of hope but scattered with pieces of a broken heart. So that was that. He had kept his distance from her when he was in town. Amelia eventually married a lawyer and moved with her new husband to Dallas. Last he heard, her parents had moved in with her and her husband. Sam heard it from Nightshade townsfolk. It embarrassed him when they asked him about her. It's true of the old saying, fate is a cruel master. At least that was how he thought about it.

The pain took its toll on Sam. His hair grew grayer and the wrinkles in his forehead grew deeper, faster since time before Amelia.

It was all turned inward where pain became energy and energy was the force he used to help forget. He worked long hours every day and sometimes into the night. All the cattle had to be rounded up from pasture to pasture in spring and fall. He mended and tended fences and animals when needed. He roped cattle, broke horses, pulled calves. In the summer and spring, he kept busy branding cattle then moving them to new grass or gathering up hay for winter. In the fall and winter, he prepared for weaning, castrating the bull calves and separating steers to round up for auction. From daylight to dusk, every day. With the help of Tom, Tom's sons and the Lowoods boys, it was a constant busyness, sunup to sundown. Sam's father and mother were hard workers even in their sunset years. They kept the ranch running smoothly right up until they both passed away. First Mrs. Anderson, then three months later, Mr. Anderson. The three ranch hands that did help were gone now. They left not long after the war broke out and never came back. There were a few stragglers that helped off and on as the war drew on, enough to keep the ranch going, but it wasn't until his father came home from war that the ranch got back to its full glory. Thankfully, Tom and Serita came along right after his folks passed, to help keep the Triple S on track as a working cattle ranch. It was life for Sam. But he wouldn't let himself think about the loneliness of that life. No, no time for that.

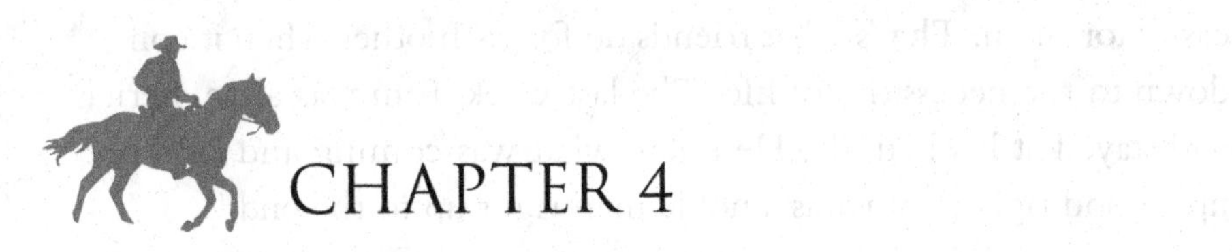

# CHAPTER 4

Serita was an integral part of the Triple S after Sam's parents were gone. Every day she shuttled back and forth from the helpers' quarters, just yards away, to the main house where he lived. His house sat up on a hilltop, while the helpers' quarters, where she and Tom lived, was on low flat, plain ground. When the leaves were gone in the fall you could just see the stone porch columns of the main house. She was taking care of two households, including him, Tom, and their sons. She worked for him every day except for holidays, half days Saturday and all day on Sunday when she took off to go to church. She saw to it that Tom and the boys were right with her at church on Sundays. That was a certain. Serita had prodded Sam to come with them, but he wasn't much for church. He could do with or without it. Not that he didn't believe in a God, he just preferred to believe from a distance. Sitting in a church pew every Sunday wasn't in his nature. Serita pestered him every week. "Gonna go to church with us on Sunday Sam?"

"Can't woman. I've got work ahead of me." was his standard excuse.

"You oughta be thinking about your soul Sam."

"My soul will take care of itself, besides the Lord knows where I'm at on Sundays. The Triple S is next thing to church as you can get." He would always thank her for the invite, then that was the end of the conversation. Tom told her to stop bugging him about it. But she never let up in fifteen years.

Tom and Serita's boys were gone now, both grown men, with

families of their own. Each had left home long before their father had gotten sick. As Tom got worse, Serita spent more time at home and less at the main house. Sam took on doing more to help make it easier for them. That's what friends do for each other when it comes down to the necessities of life. The last week Tom was alive, Serita had stayed at his bedside. He knew what was coming and he'd put up a good fight. Tom was a noble man right up to the end.

# CHAPTER 5

Before Tom got sick, Sam often invited him and Serita to the main house to share a meal. Serita did the cooking of course. It gave them a chance to talk about something other than the ranch. Usually before Christmas, or right around Thanksgiving. Never on the holiday itself, that was time left for Tom and his own family. Sam always gave them a hand full of ten-dollar bills sealed up in an envelope, just an extra bonus for the holidays. Conversations around the dinner table consisted of what the boys were doing, what the government was up to and a few humorous cowboy antidotes. Afterwards a sip of brandy in the parlor, a puff of a cigar with a kindling fire in the background, the evening ending with Serita taking home leftovers to be served for the holiday later the next day. Sam let her, the boys and Tom take the surrey home. He wouldn't think of going to the helpers' quarters to eat with them. He tried to keep from going inside their house when possible. Mostly he'd knock on their door and stay out on the porch to talk. Serita knew not to invite him in, he had declined so many times before. But when Tom died, it was the exception. He made his way back to the room where Tom was. He paid his respects, forgoing his feelings of dread and staying just long enough to comfort Serita before leaving. He thought about that a lot. Not that he didn't know how hard it was for her. He did. And so, he did his best to deal with the demons just one time for that sad occasion.

Sam was glad Tom had Serita. They were a good fit. It was the way he dreamed the life with an Amelia might have been. He didn't begrudge what Tom and Serita had. They had a good life together. Good old Tom. As kids growing up, they usually managed to find trouble when there was trouble to be had. They were more like brothers than best friends. Just two tow-headed boys struck with a similar rowdy nature. Now it was over. As his father used to say' yesterday's memories, todays realities, tomorrow the dreams to dream.'

# CHAPTER 6

Tom refused to see a doctor. Serita begged him again and again. Sam even tried to convince him. But he would only wave them off. He finally agreed to let Serita fetch Doc. Turner. By the time Doc got out to see him, Tom could no longer get out of bed. And it wasn't long after Tom took to bed that he was gone. Serita covered him in crocheted blankets she made then sent for the preacher to come pray over him. He and Tom had never seen each other shed tears growing up. They were both raised tough to the bone. They would have ribbed each other if one of them had cried about anything. But Sam couldn't help it, and he figured his old friend wouldn't have made too much of it. Same if it had been him instead. Tom Dalton was a fine man.

They buried Tom beside the rock creek on the Triple S, not far from Sam's mother and fathers' gravesite. Serita held up well. She hugged the boy's goodbye after the funeral, sending them back home to their own families. She was a strong, proud woman that didn't ask for help even though they had offered it. So it was that Sam, just one year later, waved goodbye to Serita, as she disappeared down the gangway to board the train, making way to her new life far from the Triple S. She and Star Lowoods were the only females he trusted. He was over forty now, alone, really alone for the first time in his life. Excluding himself, the bulls and stallions, the stock were the only females on the ranch now.

# CHAPTER 7

Sam Anderson was born on the Triple S late in the year 1850. Named from the initials of his great grandfather Silas, and two sons Spencer and Simon, the Triple S was a working ranch of considerable prestige. Sam's father was the last living male descendant to be raised on the ranch, that is, until Sam was born. The only time his father was away from it was when he left to be an infantry man in the Civil War. Sam could remember him dressed in rebel grays, mounting his bay mare, riding off into the countryside. Young Sam was left with his mother and three ranch hands to manage. He grew into a man then, had to. When the war was over, his father returned home to his wife and son, a changed man. He seemed to be a kinder, gentler man than before the war. Sam's mother noticed it too. In time, their lives returned to normal. And as expected, Sam, an only child, settled into the fact that he would be the one to carry on Anderson tradition. From generation to generation all the education of ranch life rolled up into a gangly teenager ready to tackle the ins and outs of the Triple S. He accepted it that was his destiny.

The original house, built by Silas and his sons, had been added on to by each generation over the years. It started out as a three-room wood shack. Gradually with the increase in money raised by selling cattle, the house was added on to every year. By the time Sam came along, it was a two-level mansion with six bedrooms upstairs, four fireplaces, a large library filled with history books, long novels, and short stories, four marble columns in the front of the house, and all the modern amenities for the time.

Triple S land was nestled near the Arkansas River bottoms between the county line of White Bluff and the hilly slopes of Miners Pass just north of Nightshade. Every year the pasture grew thick and green from seasonal fall and spring rains. Perfect for raising healthy cattle and horses. All of this now was his responsibility. Since its beginnings in 1780 the Triple S was known far and wide for its quality Angus cattle. They were a heavy and hearty stock. Rarely any trouble with calving and easily bred. All the branding, culling, foaling, calving, roping, doctoring, and hauling to town for auction was exciting for Sam when he was little. And it still was after all these years now that he was a man. It was a hard life, but he loved it. He couldn't imagine ever doing anything else but being a rancher. After his parents died, he sent word to Tom Dalton, his childhood friend, to offer him and his wife Serita, along with their two sons, the empty newlywed house. He would turn it into helpers' quarters. Tom and Serita could live there for free room and board, along with monthly pay, to help out on the ranch if they would agree to be his housekeeper and ranch hand. Sam's father helped build the home for the couple, but he wouldn't live to see, or even dream .it would never be lived in. Sam thought he would have been pleased to know that Tom was the one living there. Funny how things worked out that way.

# CHAPTER 8

The Civil war had long passed, and slavery was no longer a solution for ranch help. Not that the Anderson family had ever owned slaves. They were against the immoral practice and managed to still have a thriving cattle ranch despite the difficulty of the times. His father would never have been a part of the Confederate army if he could have had any say in the matter. Now with Tom and Serita, he had the perfect combination. All of the daily chores were divided up between Serita's two sons and her husband, Tom, with Sam coordinating the days' work. The men would set out at dawn. Working the cattle and horses every day. Tom was an organized and efficient ranch boss. His sons, Allen, and Daniel were young and strong, both putting in their time taking orders at Tom's direction. As Daniel and Allen grew to adults, both tired of ranch work and they left, first James then Daniel, moving away from ranch life to start their own families far from Nightshade. And Sam had help from the Lowoods family if he needed it.

Alvin Lowoods and family had a small farm east and within riding distance of the Triple S. They owned thirty acres planted with wheat, corn, and garden vegetables along with raising various farm animals. There were always a few hound dogs loose running around the place. The dogs were friendly, but they had a habit of running off, gone for days following a chase of rabbits or deer.

The Lowoods's harvested the farm to feed the family. They had four healthy, good-looking sons, Matthew, Mark, Luke and John, a daughter, the baby, Genesis, nicknamed Gennie. The oldest boy

Matthew was seventeen, and there was close to little more than one year apart between Mark and Luke down to the youngest son, John. Sam always joked with Alvin that if there was a fifth son, he should have been named Acts in line with the gospels of the New Testament Instead of another son they were surprised with a daughter. So, Alvin and his wife went back to the first book of the Old Testament, Genesis, and that she became. Little Gennie the last of the Lowoods. They were a close family. And just like Tom, the Lowoods were always willing to help when it counted. If the Lowoods needed a fence repaired, Sam and Tom were there to pull the barbed wire or dig a fence post. If Sam needed help with branding, or driving herds, Tom and the Lowoods pitched in. And when Tom needed help with the property around the helpers' quarters Mr. Lowoods would come and bring all the boys. Allen and Daniel were older than the Lowoods boys by five years. All of them got along and worked well together. When Sam was off to town or busy out riding the fence line, he had folks he could always depend on while he was gone. The Lowoods were good people. Neighbors weren't just neighbors, they were family.

# CHAPTER 9

Alvin Lowoods was younger than Sam by six years. He was a hard worker, a solid family man, a man of faith. He had a knack for woodworking and built most of the furniture in his house for Star, his wife. Stargazer was half English, half Cherokee. She went by the name Star and had beautiful long black silky hair, dark piercing eyes and thick sweeping eyelashes. Her skin was dark tanned, soft, and glowing. She had long slender legs and arms that moved gracefully in motion like a dance as she walked. Alvin couldn't take his eyes off her from the first day he met her and hadn't much since they married. She started having babies at eighteen, she looked like she could be an older sister rather than a mother of four, now at thirty-five. Her sons and husband doted on her. They managed the outside chores while she handled the inside. She enjoyed being outside hanging out the wash in warm weather and pumping well water for washing or bathing. Sometimes she sat in her rocking chair, carved by her husband, early in the morning before anyone was awake, just drinking coffee, reading her bible, and taking in the peacefulness of the farm. Alvin, the boys, the farm, and Gennie was her love of life. She didn't have dreams of a fancy house, or clothes. She was more comfortable in simple thin cotton print dresses that she had handmade herself. On chilly days she kept warm wearing sewn moccasins and a cowhide blanket. She was thankful that she was surrounded by growing children and a devoted husband. Alvin was a good husband, friend, father. All the children were happy and healthy. She was reminded of these things every day and it kept her heart filled with gratefulness to God.

Star kept a firm rein on the boys, but she was softer in nature to the baby, Gennie. All the boys were protective of Gennie and kept a close eye on her from the time she was born. Gennie adored her brothers. She liked to tease them or annoy them just for fun. It was just one of the pleasures of living on a farm with a pack of rowdy boys. Lots of room to run and jump, swing, swim and be free. She would have liked to have been able to go to school regularly. That was the only thing about living in the country. It was too far a ride to go to school by herself, Star explained to her. Even when her mother had agreed with it, she was only able to attend a few times a month. She had gone twice this spring and always looked forward to the next time she could go. Her mother stipulated she had to be accompanied by a brother and that was only if they didn't have to help Alvin out with farm work. Her mother would fill their pockets with cold biscuits to eat on the way. So said designated brother would saddle up the mule at dawn and off they would go, brother at the head, Gennie at the tail. Depending on the brother, James never let her drive, Matthew always did but Luke and Mark just depended on what their mood was. The time spent on the ride to school and back was mostly her talking about what she wanted to learn or what she did learn for the day. That was the worst part of the trip for brother. That girl could out talk a preacher at an all-sinners ball. The brother would sit in school for the day, sometimes to learn, but most times just waiting for it to be over. None of the boys were up for an education. After all their mother had taught them the important things at home. Their education was what they learned working on the farm. After school was over, they made their way back home, Gennie carried away in conversation of school and farm stories. Both were always ready for a hot meal, and bed.

# CHAPTER 10

Star's mother was English. Her father Cherokee. They met each other in 1840 at the cattle auction in Nightshade. Star's mother was standing there watching the lines of cowboy's ride by. She was propped up against the cattle chute when she had the feeling that someone was staring at her. As she made her way around the cattle chute to see who was standing behind the panels, she ran face to face into Nekota Starcatcher. Both startled each other. It was a struggling conversation to begin with but by the end of the auction, they found that it was more than just a new friendship that was growing. Nekota was full Cherokee, and he spoke both English and Iroquoian. He liked the way her voice sounded, so different from the local girls. She was poised and very educated. They spent every day together since the auction. Much to the surprise of the parents, six weeks later, he asked permission for her hand, such as was the style in English tradition. Despite protests from the parents on both sides of the family, they relented. Two months later a preacher friend of the family married them. The new couple settled in on their own land with just a red heifer calve and an old blind bull Nekota had bought at the auction that same day. Star's mother had been educated in the finest schools in England from a very young age. She was determined that her children would learn to read and write just as she had. So, Star and her brothers and sisters received an English education. She was taught to read from the Bible, and it continued right up until the day her mother died. Star was only sixteen. By then she was fluent in reading, speaking in English and Iroquoian her father's native tongue. She had a little of her mother's Cockney accent, mixed in with southern drawl. By seventeen she had met Alvin Lowoods, married, and moved on with Alvin to his small farm just two miles east of the Triple S. At eighteen the babies started coming. She and Alvin worked hard to manage the farm. Every morning up at dawn her and Alvin read the bible together. Then out to check the livestock of pigs, goats, a milk cow, mules, and chickens. Everything had to be fed, drawn water from the well to tote to the water troughs, gather eggs, cow and goats milked then in for a hot breakfast and back out again to rake or put-up hay in the barn, muck the stalls, make barn repairs then back in for lunch. After lunch, milk cows and goats again before evening, and mules brought in from pasture to the barn for hoof trimming and stalled for the night. In the summer Alvin and Star did a little fishing before dinner. Once a week in the winter, they hunted for deer, squirrels, or game birds. In the spring, Alvin hitched up the mules and broke ground for planting. They had corn, beans, potatoes, turnips, for food. As the children came along each one was added into the farm chores based on their ability to help. Their responsibilities grew as they got older and were able to take on more chores.

Star delivered all her children at home in the four-poster bed that Alvin had built and carved for her. Alvin delivered all the babies. He had helped birth many cows and pigs, so he had some idea of what to expect. It was still a big worry for him as Star was the light of his life. But after Matthew was born, he was more at ease as the other babies came along. All the boys were delivered in the spring, but Gennie came late in the fall. Star, like her mother, read the Bible to each child from birth and taught all of them to read and write with some basic number studies added in later. School was in town, and it would have been difficult to send the children to school every day since the farm had to be tended to and they needed to help out with the neighbor's ranch at the Triple S. But with Gennie, she made the allowances so that she could attend school although it wasn't regular.

Alvin and Star met Sam after the birth of their first son. Alvin had stopped by the Triple S to ask for directions to Doc Turner's house since he was worried about the welfare of his wife and new son. Sam drove Alvin to Doc Turner collecting him in the buckboard then bringing them both back to their homes once it was confirmed mother and baby were both strong and healthy. Since that day, both Alvin and Sam were connected by their love of the land and mutual respect. Sam butchered a steer every year in the fall and split the meat with Alvin. Sam also gave Tom and Serita a side of meat every year too. Everything had its place and a place for everything.

# CHAPTER 11

Serita hounded Sam for years to find a woman and get married. It was always the same. "What are ya waiting for Sam, judgement day?" She meant the best for him, but he just couldn't bring himself to take the time, nor did he have the desire to make time. Staying busy on the ranch made the time pass so fast he hadn't noticed he was getting older. Serita came every day to cook and clean for him and he had done fine without a woman until now. Sam was content with life, as is. Serita, Tom, and the boys were his family. Now that Tom had passed, he was alone again. He missed his friend Tom. They had so many memories growing up together. He would always be thankful for that.

When Tom died, Sam offered to give Serita the house and the land to her, but she refused. Her sister needed her, and she needed to be with her own family again. The last few weeks that Sam saw her she was constantly nagging him about finding a housekeeper. She suggested he put an ad in the Nightshade Editor for a housekeeper. She continued to warn him she would be leaving in due time, and he was going to need some help. But Sam wasn't so sure Serita was right about that. At, least up to now.

Now it had been four weeks since she left, and he figured there might have been something to that ad thing. It might not be a bad idea to take her up on her advice. He had burnt his supper the last four nights in a row and was getting tired of stale bread, jerky and coffee for dinner, breakfast, and lunch. His socks had holes, he didn't have a clean shirt and he needed to get food supplies but was not sure of how much or many. He could manage the workings of the ranch but what about which soap was for clothes and which for dishes? Such trivial things. He could figure it out eventually, but did he really want to?

# CHAPTER 12

HOUSEKEEPER WANTED AT TRIPLE S RANCH. ROOM AND BOARD INCLUDED. SEE GROVER CHAMBERS AR NIGHTSHADE EDITOR

Yes, he would take the note to town in the morning when he drove the cattle in and place the ad. Maybe in a few weeks there would be more than just stale bread and coffee for meals. The boys had helped Serita move out of the helpers' quarters, but Sam drove her to the train station in Jonesboro. Sam took the buckboard full of Serita's things and the two of them headed out to town, hardly saying a word all the way to Nightshade. She hugged him as she boarded the train and reminded him once again, he needed to find a new housekeeper. He felt that old feeling of pain again as he waved goodbye. Serita had been like a mother bird to him. Always there to keep him going. When driving home he stopped again at the house where both Tom, Serita and the boys lived. He had a strange feeling when he went to the house this time. Seeing it empty again after so long was like returning to the grave of a loved one. That sad and silent ghostly feeling. It had been twenty years since he had built that house for his bride to be. But he shrugged it off thinking he was too old for sad sentiments at his age. He could see the linens, new curtains, and the painted walls from the windows as he passed. They had made it a home for raising kids in and growing old together. It was a different house now. It might be a nice to have someone living there again soon

# CHAPTER 13

Sam Anderson couldn't understand why anyone would want to live in a dusty old town with people bustling about everywhere talking incessantly about the latest news and gossips. He was used to the quiet out on the ranch. There, the calls of the heifers to their calves and sounds of crickets, birds and frogs were the only interruptions of peace to be heard. Other than the Daltons, you couldn't walk a mile either way and see a person or hear a human voice out in the open country. The most conversation he had was talking to Tom and Serita or, when he would ride over to the Lowoods occasionally to either offer help with their farm or ask for help from the boys. They were a rowdy bunch of boys, which included Gennie buttin' in right in the middle of them. He wouldn't have been able to get a word in sideways as far as conversation, but he didn't let it bother him too much.

They sure were a busy sort.

Sam went to Nightshade every three months for supplies and twice a year to sell cattle at the market. Nightshade was the nearest weigh station for livestock. There were always people in the streets and open markets with vendors for produce, housewares, or liquid refreshments. Sam rarely patronized the vendors but once he did buy a pocketknife there after he realized he had lost his on the ride to town. It was a flashy piece of steel with an eagle engraved on the blade and a solid black handle. The blade had worn down over time by cutting everything from cow hides to peeling apples. Now he could barely make out the eagle's wing.

The people of Nightshade were too nosey for Sam's taste. Seems like they were always fishin' around for information too personal for an average rancher or ranch hand. These were Amelia's kind of folk. Not his. There was a post office just coming into town on the east side which included a telegraph machine. Old man Barney ran the telegraph and sorted the mail. He knew everybody's business by reading all the post cards sent from outside or to Nightshade He always made a point to ask about Aunt Martha's vacation to the beach in Spain or if Mr. Henry liked his fishing trip with his son-in-law in Georgia. Mr. Barney also was the first one in the Wellburn family to know that Mr. Wellburn's daughter from Minnesota had twins. Of course, he kept up to date on all the news from in and out of town whenever anyone needed to send or receive a telegraph.

The Royal Inn Hotel was north of town, and it offered a room with a hot bath for two dollars a night. Extra two dollars if you're a lonely man needing a night visit. A saloon built next door to the hotel was accessible to drunks and dusty cowpokes. The banging out of piano music from the bar could easily be heard every night from the top to bottom floors of the hotel. If you were a sound sleeper it didn't matter but those that don't care for such noise would bury their head in their pillows until the music died which sometimes carried on until daylight.

A livery on the south side of the street was available for fresh horses to buy or sell. Tack was usually included in the deal, but it really wasn't much of a deal as most of the saddles were worn out with broken saddle horns and a cheap bridle added into the sale.

The stockyards were just past the livery with all the smells that would lead you right to it just in case you needed directions.

The train station and the bank were on the east edges of town, with a notary in the bank basement for anybody needing legal paperwork completed. Doc Turner kept a small medical office behind the station, but he rarely did much doctoring. He was well into his eighties and most of the townsfolk pretty much used their own homemade remedies unless it was prudent due to Doc's hard of hearing.

A small school was just out of Nightshade city limits. It was a two-room building with one large window and a wood swing on the only tree in town. Miss Tanner, the town spinster was the school marm and had been for twenty-five years. She was known to keep a box of thin reed switches next to her desk. Many a rambunctious boy was familiar with the sharp end of those reeds occasionally.

A small church and graveyard sat just west of the school. It had a large steeple with a church bell that could be heard for a country mile on Sunday mornings. This is the church that both Serita and the Lowoods attended every Sunday. Plenty of weddings and funerals of Nightshade members were had there. All performed by the Reverend Marcus Mayweather, for a nominal contribution to the church of course.

The Sheriff's office and jail were on the west side of town. There usually was a cell or two that housed a drunk or a rowdy cowboy for a one or two-night stay. The sheriff and his deputy took turns on duty. Not much illegal activity in Nightshade other than the town drunks and a weekly bar fight. Upstairs behind the old dentist office was the Arkansas Nightshade Editor. The paper had been printing news since the Civil War began. There was one printing press for all the towns north of the Arkansas River. Grover Chambers was the printing press owner. The first newspaper ever printed in the Editor was the news about the death of President Lincoln. That paper sold out in less than two hours. Grover said the death of Lincoln made him a wealthy man, sad to say. In a rural area with just under six hundred people that was the first and last time all the papers had completely sold out. Since then, the main attraction had been local news, sales ads, and gossip columns as such the town had plenty of subjects to include.

The only other businesses were the general store for clothing, books, canned goods and various merchandise available to townsfolk every day except on Sunday. Even people from Little Rock and on the outskirts of town met regularly there to engage in commerce or, like most of the husbands in town, a good competitive game of checkers. The proprietor had arranged a checkers table, made from wood sawhorses and cedar barrels. Mainly it was made to bide the time for men as their wives and other women shopped. The game stayed uninterrupted as the womenfolk wandered over to the Nightshade Dress and Petticoat shop just across the street. There were always fancy dresses and matching bonnets placed right in front of the shop window to attract customers as they strolled by. The two sisters that owned the shop were kept in high regard as master salesmen. Not many women made it out of the store without a purchase. The sisters were on a first name basis with almost all the women from Nightshade and it's surrounding areas.

Twice a year Sam brought half his herd into town. He rounded up the yearlings first, then the older steers. Tom, his sons, and a few or all the Lowoods boys, helped drive in the cattle to town, each receiving their pay out of the earnings Sam collected from auction. The Lowoods had money of their own from selling the harvest from the farm, but it wasn't much. Sam let them use the buckboard to haul the stacks of wheat and corn to town. After auction, he would walk to the bank and deposit the remainder of his earnings. He didn't like keeping large sums of money on him or at the ranch. And he always had his pistols with him, loaded, just in case. His father had an account already set up when he took over the Triple S, so Sam just continued the practice. He kept what he needed in his satchel and used the rest to pay the boys or buy supplies. They all spent their pay at the mercantile on sundries, supplies, and farm goods. None of the boys or Tom stayed the night in town. Their women folk wouldn't have it. Serita had told him when men are together in a pack it's a sure time for trouble in a town looking for it. Star had said the same thing to Alvin. They all would start the trip back home after a few hours of spending money and after engaging in some small talk with the locals. Once after an auction, a thunderstorm came up so hard it rained solid for five hours, but the boys just pulled out their ponchos and huddled inside the livery until the rain let up. They left town on their horses kicking up the mud as they trampled through the puddles on the way home.

Sam's bank account had grown steadily over the years. He wasn't much on spending. He wasn't rich but he was comfortably well off. Walking down the streets of Nightshade he made the occasional pleasantries such as good morning and how are yous to the few people he made eye contact with, tipping his hat to the ladies, and nodding to the men out of mannerly respect.

But he tried to make each stay in town as short as possible. As soon as he finished what business he had he made his way back home, sometimes with the boys, sometimes alone.

The years had taken their toll on Sam. His skin was dry as leather with a few deep wrinkles, tanned and tall. Working out in the sun all day makes a man tough. His hair was still mostly coal black, just a few gray hairs around his ears were noticeable when the light hit just right. His smile covered most of his face the few times he did smile. He got his green eyes from his father. Handed down over the years from the original Anderson family. He had strong rough hands with long lean fingers. Many times, used to wrangle a steer or pull a calf in trouble. Sam began to notice he had gained a little thickness around his hips this past year. All Serita's good cooking had caught up to him. He wore his belt a little looser to keep up his working denims. He was still as strong as a horse even at forty-one. He could ride in a saddle tall and lean all day without a sore bone or muscle in his body. A handsome strong face with weathered green eyes, Sam would never have issues getting looks from women though he never entertained the notion. Though most women had already married and had families by the time he was in his early thirties. At twenty-one he had found love only to lose it before he turned twenty-three years old. From then on, he was his own man no need for women in his life. Just work hard from dawn to dusk day after day.

So today he and the Lowoods boys came into town with the cattle, he pulled up his horse to the hitching post, wrapped the reins around it twice and headed up the street to the Nightshade Editor. Climbing the stairs, he slowly reached into his right pocket to be sure he still had the paper from this morning. "How ya doin' these days Mr. Anderson?" Grover Chambers walked over from behind the printing press with his leather apron covered in dust. He wore a pair of wire rimmed glasses, along with a worn-down pencil flecked with tiny ink spots, that lay perched behind his ear. He held out his hand to Sam to greet him. Sam gripped Mr. Chambers' hand firmly within his cupping his other hand over the held out offering of Grover Chambers.

"I'm lookin' for some help on the ranch Mr. Chambers."

"Call me Grover Mr. Anderson. How can I help?"

"Well, I guess you better call me Sam then Grover if we're gonna be on a first name callin' basis. I gotta want ad here that I'd like to put in your paper as soon as ya can." Sam released his grip from Mr. Chambers and pulled out the paper from his pocket.

"Well let's have a look at what ya got there." Grover pulled the pencil out from behind his ear and read the words aloud, which made Sam a little uneasy. "So, you needin' a new housekeeper there huh Sam? Serita was a mighty fine woman. Gonna be hard to find someone to replace what she done for ya."

His uneasiness passed, Sam replied, "Yeah, I wasn't really thinkin' about hirin' anybody, but Serita kept poundin' on me to get someone. To tell you the truth, I can't cook too well and the housekeepin' chores just don't seem to be gettin' done rightly. So, thought I'd try and get someone to come out to the ranch to help out."

Grover rubbed his chin for a minute and said "Gonna cost you about a dollar. I can run it starting tomorrow and every day for one full month. If you need more time in the paper, you'll have to come back and pay another dollar."

Sam nodded. "One month oughta do." He pulled out the silver dollar from his left pocket and handed it to Grover. They shook hands once more to seal the deal.

As Sam was walking out the door, Grover yelled. "Good Luck to ya Sam! Hope you find someone half as good as Serita!" Sam waved, and slowly made his way down the stairs and back outside to the hitching post. Not much luck he would ever find someone like Serita. He swung into the saddle then kicked his horse riding back through town to meet up with the Lowoods. He and the boys headed on back to the Triple S.

# CHAPTER 14

She was only planning to visit for a short time in Nightshade. Her cousin, Naomi, had encouraged her to bring Jacob with her and stay for at least until she could find a job. Hannah had so many things to think about. What would she do for work? How could she make a living and take care of her son? Jacob was only nine years old, but he was much older than his years. He had been the little man of the house now since his father had passed last summer. Jack, his father, hadn't been the best at saving money nor at helping out with keeping a house together. Hannah did the best she could, but now she was desperate. Moving from West Virginia to Arkansas had not been in the plan. She thought she, Jack and Jacob would live in their little house until they had enough money to buy it. But Jack couldn't even keep sporadic work as a handyman and many times he would spend what he did earn on whiskey at the saloon. Hannah believed God was going to provide no matter how sparse it got. Now she was beginning to wonder was this what God had in mind? Did he mean for her to be destitute and leave her wondering where the next meal was coming from or if, for that matter, would they even have a roof over their heads? Hannah had prayed so long for an answer even before Jack died. She was losing faith and hope. Now she didn't know what she should pray for so she just prayed that God would give her hope. He would have to work it out because she was getting tired of looking for answers.

Naomi had her husband and two daughters to think of. It's true she did have the room. They lived in a large fine home in

Nightshade city limits. Naomi's husband was a dentist and he also had inherited money from his wealthy parents. When Naomi learned that her cousin, Hannah was going to be living in the street with her nine-year-old son, she quickly sent word for her to come stay as long as she needed. Naomi sent train fare for both Hannah and Jack to travel to Nightshade.

Hannah was humbled by her cousin's generosity. She had little to pack when she left West Virginia. Just a few clothes for her and Jack. She had two dollars left and a little bit of food which she packed in a small lunch pail to make the trip to Arkansas. "God is making a way for us Jacob. We just gotta keep on praying and wait for the answers to come."

"I know he will mama, I'm gonna help God take good care of you."

Eight months had passed quickly since she moved in with Naomi. Hannah kept a close eye on the paper for want ads and she had been asking around town if anyone needed the help of a seamstress or cook. She had worked a few jobs for people that needed alterations for their growing children's play clothes. But it wasn't anything steady that she could count on. Jacob was back in school at least; he was getting along well with the move so far.

Hannah had learned how to sew and cook at an early age. She had plenty of practice with her sisters and brothers. A family of nine requires lots of cooking, cleaning, and sewing. Hannah was the youngest, but she was quick to accomplish those skills. Between her four brothers and two sisters there was always time to practice on each other. Her parents made sure they all could survive the world when it came down to it. At the time she met Jack, she was cooking and delivering meals to the sick people in the congregation of the church. It was something that her mother had instilled in all the children." When you help others, you're helping yourself and your bind with God gets tighter," just one of several life lessons their mother had taught them.

They all learned that blessing others was a gift from God. It's something that her mother and father both lived.

Jack was visiting his friend's sick mother when Hannah arrived. She had a basket full of fresh baked bread, corn fritters, baked beans, and homemade apple pie. Jack liked the smell of baked bread, but he was more than interested in the girl that brought them. Hannah wore a dark green pinafore with a crisp white blouse. She had her long auburn hair pulled back with a green ribbon that matched the pinafore. With her dark blue eyes and her creamy white skin, she looked more like a porcelain doll rather than a young girl of eighteen. She was a little on the thin side but not in the areas that counted. And she had pretty hands, the kind that hadn't been exposed to the sun all day as many women working in the fields had. Jack stared at her longer than he realized, causing Hannah's cheeks to glow with a faint blush. She smiled at him, and he could see the tiny little dimples around her full lips. He nervously stood up from the chair that he was sitting in and took his hat off his head, holding it firmly between his fingers hoping that would stop his hands from shaking. More hoping that she wouldn't notice. She was the most beautiful girl he had seen in the whole state of Virginia, and he had been around enough girls to be an expert on that subject.

"Hello, mam my name is Jack Martin, I'm here visiting Ms. Truel. My friend Peter, her son, works with me on a shipping barge but I'm on leave so he asked me to check on his mother when I was in town. I didn't realize she had become ill until I saw her today."

"Jack, I'm much better so when you see Peter again you can tell him about my good friends from the church who are taking care of me. Really, I'm feeling much better, and Hannah is so kind to bring me this lovely meal today."

"Glad to hear it Ms. Truel, I didn't know you were having company, or I would have brought this over earlier. Really, it's nothing, we had some corn fritters and bread left over and no one in my house likes apple pie like I do so I just thought you might enjoy it."

"Jack, would you like a piece of pie? Hannah is a very good cook. You can ask anyone."

"Oh, I don't' know Ms. Truel, it looks and smells wonderful, but Ms. Hannah made this just for you."

"Mr. Jack, I don't mind if Ms. Truel doesn't. After all there will be plenty left over if you'd like for me to cut you a piece."

"No mister, just Jack, please mam. I'd be obliged then to try a piece of homemade apple pie."

At the time Hannah couldn't have known how her life would have changed. They married a year later, then the year after that Jacob came along. Jack worked on shipping boats for the first two years of their marriage. He was at sea for several months at a time. But each time he came home, he was different than the time before. She still loved him; she just didn't know how he could be so different than when they first met. It was like living with a stranger for a while. Some days they were fine. Some days, well, she wondered. The long bouts at sea meant Hannah was raising Jacob alone. Her family helped as much as they could. Naomi as well. But Hannah preferred to go it by herself. She was too proud to depend on anyone else, besides her parents had brought her up to know how to take care of herself. Each time Jack came home from the sea, he would be a loving husband and father. Just for a while. As time went on, he began frequenting the saloons more and more, coming home late in a drunken stupor. He eventually lost work on the ship, and after that he was rarely sober. Hannah did the best[1] she could make do with the little amount of money she had saved. Jacob, even as a young boy, saw the toll his father's drinking took on his mother. He tried to keep up with the tasks around the house. All the while attending school daily, but it was getting too much for him and he was no longer able to stay in school. Finally, one winter night, Jack went to bed soggy drunk and never woke up again. It was a challenging time for them. Hannah had been raising her son with no help from Jack for a long time. Now it was permanently so.

# CHAPTER 15

As children, Naomi and Hannah weren't just cousins. They were best friends. Inseparable. Where one was the other was or at least not far behind. Just two spirited little girls sharing secrets, hopes and dreams together. They both had grown up to be solid core of the earth women. Hannah was there for Naomi when she married her husband, had her babies and for the move to Arkansas. Naomi was there for Hannah when she married Jack and when Jacob was born. Though Hannah refused more often than not, Naomi insisted to help while Jack was at sea.

Naomi's husband, Robert, took a job in Arkansas to open a dental office. Naomi, Robert, and their daughters left out on the train early one morning, leaving West Virginia and Hannah behind. They hugged each other tightly, then Naomi boarded the train waving goodbye until the train was no longer in sight. Over time they kept in touch. Letters were sent to and from on a regular basis. Naomi had always been concerned about Jack's drinking, seeing for herself what he could be like. She made Hannah promise that if times got too hard, she would leave him and bring Jacob with her to Arkansas.

So now, here she was. Living with Naomi and her family, thinking about what she could do to provide for her son.

And so it was that she noticed a small ad in the Nightshade Editor one spring morning while sitting on Naomi's porch swing.

# CHAPTER 16

HOUSEKEEPER WANTED FOR TRIPLE S RANCH. ROOM AND BOARD INCLUDED. SEE GROVER CHAMBERS AT AR NIGHTSHADE EDITOR.

Housekeeper on a ranch? Room and board? This could be an answered prayer by way of the want ads. She would talk to Naomi about it. Of course, she would need more information first. Hannah thought about going into town the next day to ask about it. Yes, she would definitely check on it first thing tomorrow. Then she'd sit down with Naomi to get her advice. She wouldn't get her hopes up though. There were so many things to consider. Who placed the ad for one thing? And how would they feel about her bringing her son? Where was the ranch located? Would Jacob still be able to attend school? There she goes again trying to out God, God. She just had to learn that if this was God's plan, then it meant she didn't need to worry.

Hannah went to bed hopeful for the next day. Already God had answered her prayer by giving her hope back. She thanked him under her breath silently and slept soundly for the first time in a while.

Next morning, she was up cooking breakfast for Naomi and the girls. Robert had already left for work. "You seem rested this morning, Hannah."

"I'm feeling better today, Naomi. I think I'll go into town for a little while, after getting Jacob off to school. There're a few things I'd like to see about, some possible job offers."

Naomi looked up from her coffee cup with a puzzled face. "Oh, you have something in mind?" Hannah stopped wringing the apron between her hands and sat down beside Naomi.

"Well, just a few possibilities. But not anything definite. I thought it wouldn't hurt to see if there was something I could do that would give me a chance to save some money. Maybe I could find me and Jacob a place of our own. It would take the burden off of you and Robert."

Naomi shook her head, "Hannah, what did I tell you, you aren't obligated to us for anything. We are family and you shouldn't be beholden to family. When you're able, you'll find work, but until then, your priority is keeping a stable home for Jacob. Afterall. You take care of so many things for us, too much. I rarely have housework to do because you're up early and it's all done before I even get out of bed. The girls are even helping me more seeing all that you do. That's worth a lot more than just giving you a free room with meals."

"It helps me keep my mind off my troubles, Naomi. The day goes by so fast that I don't have time to think about the little nagging thoughts in my head. Besides, I hadn't planned on staying a long time here if I could help it. Jacob and I need our own place. Nothing fancy, but someplace he could grow up in and have a place to call home. That's what I hope for anyway."

"Oh, I understand completely Hannah. Just know you are welcome to stay as long as you need. I know you need your own space. Just be patient and trust. The Lord knows your heart."

Hannah finished serving and eating breakfast. Naomi helped her wash the dishes as they talked about details of the day while cleaning up the kitchen. Jacob was ready, so Hannah grabbed her overcoat and headed out the door to walk him to school. She had a few hours free to go by the AR Nightshade Editor and inquire about the housekeeper ad. After that, she could start making a plan.

Hannah climbed the stairs to the Nightshade Editor office, holding the piece of paper she had cut out of the want ads section. When she walked into the office, she saw a man standing behind the counter talking to an older man with wire rimmed glasses, a dusty apron, and a pencil behind his ear. As both men ended their conversation, the younger man turned and left the office tipping his hat to Hannah as he walked away. Hannah leaned against the counter and handed the paper to Mr. Chambers. "Good morning, sir. I was wondering, can you tell me anything about this ad? Is the job still available?"

Grover read the paper under his breath then looked up and said" Yes mam. Far as I know it is. Are you interested in the position?"

"Well can you tell me much about it? I'm Hannah Martin. I have a few questions."

"Names Grover mam, nice to meet ya, you're fairly new in town, aren't ya?"

"Yes, Mr. Grover, I've been staying with my cousin, Naomi, her husband Robert, he's the new dentist from West Virginia."

Grover knew of him. "Yeah, I need to get over there and introduce myself to him, got a few teeth that's been botherin' me. We hadn't had a dentist in town for quite a while you know, so it's pretty good news for Nightshade."

Hannah pressed him, "This ranch, is it near town here?"

"Well, it's not too far but it ain't near neither." 'Bout fifteen miles south of Nightshade on eight hundred acres of land. Called the Triple S: It's about a three-hour buggy ride in good weather, ten when it's bad. So, ya think you might be interested?"

Hannah nodded, "Yes sir, I might be, do you know who the person is that placed the ad?"

"Well now, I've had a distant knowledge of him over the years and all his goin' ons in life. He's been on his own since he lost his ranch boss then the housekeeper."

"Came in her last month wantin' to put this ad in for a housekeeper. I guess that's how you seen it?"

"Yes, it sounds like something I could do, a man huh? Any idea about the details of the job?"

"Well, man's name is Sam Anderson, he owns the ranch and has worked it since he was a little bit of a thing. Up until his parents passed, he didn't need any help. But when they passed, his old friend

Tom and his wife Serita helped keep it ah runnin.' They lived in the house you'd be in, if ya get the job. Tom died about a year ago and then Serita moved away to Kansas a few weeks ago. Ole Sam thought he could handle the house and the ranch, but he's gotten a little sideways on the housekeepin' part, so he came in here a few weeks ago, puttin' in this want ad for a housekeeper. I gotta tell ya, he's a hardheaded cowboy and it took him a bit to admit he couldn't do it all."

"Do you have an idea of what the job duties are?"

"Well now you would have to talk to Sam about that, but I suspect you would just be takin' over in Serita's place. She done the cookin and the cleanin', washin', shoppin' for groceries, writin' letters, keepin' ledgers up to date, sewin', cannin' and cuttin' hair. You better talk to Sam about all that though."

"Room and board included?"

"Yep, nice house too, Sam built that thing years ago when he was gonna get married, but it didn't work out for him. I probably shouldn't be mentionin' that, but word gets around here ya know. And it's kinda my business, me bein' the only newspaper man in town. It's a funny thing Sam never tore it down. But just as well, he turned it into a helper's quarters, be perfect for someone to make it into a home again."

"How do I get in touch with Mr. Sam?"

"Sam Anderson mam. Well, you go over to the post office and send back a response to the ad then ya have Mr. Barney get it out in the mail. Takes a day or two before it'll get to Sam. Likely you'd see him pretty soon anyways, as he's due in town again for supplies. And too he shows up twice a year drivin' in the cattle for auction. Sounds like it could be just the job for ya. Had a lady in here a few weeks ago that checked into it but that didn't work out."

"Ok, well I'll get over to see Mr. Barney and find out when he can send it out for me. Do I owe you anything Mr. Grover?"

'Nope, not a thing, just keep in touch. I like to keep up with my customers." Hannah wrote down her contact information and gave it to Grover then headed back out the door. But, having second thoughts she turned back for one more question.

"Mr. Grover? Just what kind of man is this, Sam Anderson?" Grover slowly bent his head rubbing his chin with one finger,

"Well, he's not much a man of words, and pretty grumpy at times, but overall, a real sober man, strong, proud, though some folks around here call him stubborn as a Charleston mule. I reckon hard times in life can change your nature, nothin' wrong with that, everybody's got their own way about it. Of course, you'll have to decide that for yourself when you meet him. Sam is Sam, you can depend on that for whatever it's worth to ya. You keep that in mind, and you'll be alight, Good luck to you Mrs. Martin."

Hannah made her way up the street to the postmaster. Mr. Barney didn't notice her when she came in, he was too busy reading a new postcard from Ohio. Hannah forced a mild cough to catch his attention.

"Excuse me mam, I didn't hear you come in, what can I do you for?"

"I'd like to send a letter in reply to a want ad. I'd like to send it as soon as possible."

"Ok, let me get my pencil and paper and we'll fix ya right up."

# CHAPTER 17

Sam thumbed through the mail to see which to keep and which to throw away. He had just sat down at the kitchen table with his second cup of coffee for the morning. Yesterday he made the trip to Nightshade for supplies and picked up his mail from Mr. Barney. Gonna be another nice one today looks like. He planned on checking the north pasture to see how the hay situation might be, maybe try and get another cuttin' in before the end of summer. He would ride down to the Lowoods later and see if the boys would be able to come and help get in a few bales before sundown.

One letter caught his attention. It was post marked from Nightshade.

He'd only had one response in almost a month of placing the ad. It was from an elderly woman that only wanted to work until her daughter moved out of town. Sam had met her at the Editor, and she seemed nice, but he didn't like the idea that in a few months he might have to start looking for help all over again. He wanted something a little more dependable. This could be promising.

Mrs. Hannah Martin Care of AR Nightshade Editor, to Mr. Sam Anderson:

Dear Mr. Anderson,

I am responding to the ad you placed three weeks ago in the Editor. Currently I am living with my cousin in Nightshade. I am interested in the housekeeper position you posted. I am experienced in cooking, sewing and taking care of a home. Please contact Grover Chambers to meet me in person if you are still in need of help. I look forward to hearing from you. Thank you. Sincerely, Mrs. Hannah Martin.

Must be a widow woman since it was signed Mrs. He couldn't imagine if she was married, why the husband didn't do the writin'. And she hadn't mentioned anything about family in the letter. He would ride to town in the mornin' to visit Grover at the Editor. By tomorrow, he might even be sittin' down to a regular meal. Just thinkin' about that made his stomach growl. If things worked out could be just the answer, he'd been waitin' on.

Sam got up early and gathered his list of supplies for the month. He guessed he ought to try and look presentable since manners required it for meeting a lady. He had taken a bath, shaved and put on his last clean shirt for the week. He decided to wear his new boots with his dark denims. Looking at himself in the mirror, he thought it was not bad. He didn't want to look too citied up, that might lead to a wrong first impression, though it couldn't hurt to look favorable. He needed a housekeeper and whatever he could do to put things in his favor would be best. He was still a little tired from putting up hay yesterday. Altogether, he and the Lowoods put up two hundred bales in the barn. He sent them home with twenty to feed their own animals. He'd spare them a few more if they wanted it. Gennie had come with them, but she only stayed to watch them rake, then she rode back home to help Star fix supper. It was going to be a nice day for the ride into town. He was looking forward to getting a new housekeeper. Of course, he didn't expect the new lady to meet up to Serita's qualities. But it could be an agreeable situation. After all, this Mrs. Martin, might decide she didn't want the job. So, he decided not to dwell on future possibilities.

He harnessed up the mules, climbed up in the buckboard and set out to Nightshade. The ride to and from town was when Sam did most of his thinking. Anytime he had a worry or doubts, the few hours behind a team of mules were the place he could let it go. Of course, ridin' the Triple S was the best place for a man to think. Things just didn't seem so big when you're ridin' along an old wagon road, with blue skies, warm sunshine and the rhythm of hooves clicking on the ground. It seemed a shorter trip to town today for some reason. He must have had more on his mind than he realized.

In town Sam finished up gathering the supplies and loaded them into the back of buckboard. With that done, he headed up to the Editor to talk to Grover about the response to his ad.

"Well Grover, do you think this lady is really interested in the job".

"I think she is Sam". She seemed to have a lot of questions about it, so that tells me she means business."

"How do I go about meetin' with her Grover?"

"I got the information right here Sam. She's kin to the new dentist in town." Grover handed Sam a piece of paper with Hannah's information.

"Preciate, it Grover. I'll let you know in a bit if I need that ad stopped or not."

He waved goodbye to Grover, curious to see what this Mrs. Martin would be like.

Sam knocked on the door of the home of Naomi and Robert Sanders MD, DDS. He was surprised to see the door open and a child standing in front of him. "Is your mother home son?"

The boy looked at him, puzzled at a stranger asking about his mother. "Who are you mister?"

'Names Sam Anderson, I'm looking for a Mrs. Hannah Martin, does she live here?"

"Umm yes sir, ok. Just a minute." And with that the boy closed the door, leaving Sam to wonder if he was wasting his time on this venture. A few minutes went by before the door opened again, this time a woman in a green dress and full petticoat answered. "Hello, can I help you?'

"Are you Mrs. Martin?"

"Oh no, I'm Naomi, Mrs. Martin's cousin, if you'll come in, I'll have her come down. You must be Mr. Anderson. I'm sorry about Jacob's manners, I'm afraid he's still got a little more to learn about greeting someone at the door."

"It's quite all right mam, no harm done."

"Hannah told me she answered your ad. Just follow me into the parlor and I'll seat you in there, please."

She led him past a column of stairs and a wall with pictures of children, a man, and the woman he was following to the parlor. He didn't see any pictures of the boy that met him at the door. He guessed maybe there were more pictures somewhere of him in another place in the house. Naomi brought him to a tapestry sofa and motioned for him to sit.

"Can I get you something to drink while you wait, Mr. Anderson?"

"Oh no thank you mam. I'm fine."

Sam heard Naomi call down for Hannah. She thanked Naomi quietly then made her way to the parlor. When he saw her walking towards him, he stood up from being seated as it wouldn't have been a polite greeting for a man to stay seated in a lady's presence. He couldn't help but notice how pretty she was. She had long shiny auburn hair that fell loosely around her shoulders. Her hair reminded him of the color of a newborn chestnut calf he pulled a few days back. It's rich and deep reddish-brown hue which made her eyes look bluer than blue. Her face was pleasing to look at with full lips and a simple but genuine smile. She looked a little on the thin side but that just meant to him she was likely to be a spry, active woman. He stood up to greet her by removing his cowboy hat, holding it by the brim with both hands. Next to his six- foot four frame she seemed like a tiny doll. He had to look down to her to stay eye level.

She held out her hand to him and he squeezed it just a little bit, hoping he hadn't squeezed too hard.

Sam had pictured in his mind how he thought she would look but this was not what he expected. In his mind Mrs. Martin would have been a plump, elderly lady with gray hair and a bustle. Kinda of like the other lady that responded to his ad. Looks like Grover left out some important details.

"Please sit-down sir. Make yourself comfortable."

As they both took their seats in the parlor, Sam placed his hat beside him on the sofa. He ran his fingers through his hair to keep the loose ends in place, trying to act as if that was a normal thing for him to do. Hannah sat across from him in a chair in front of the fireplace.

"I'm Mrs. Hannah Martin. Are you the person that is looking to hire a housekeeper?"

"Ah, yes mam, Sam Anderson, I'm the one. Grover gave me your information; I hope you don't mind that I called on you today. I just wanted to make sure you wanted the job."

"Oh yes, I do, and it's fine that you called on me. Mr. Grover told me you might be coming into town soon to get your supplies so I was hoping I would meet you. Can you tell me a little more about what you're needing?"

"Well I live in a large home on a cattle ranch and I'm needin' some help with the cleanin, and cookin meals. Livin 'on a ranch is a little different, it's not like town livin' if that's what you're looking for. If you're interested, I'd expect you to keep up with grocery items and give me a list of supplies for three months. You can either come with me to town for supplies or I can just get 'em when I'm here. There may be times you have to do secretarial things, like write letters or correspondence. Some sewin, launderin' and general housework is also expected. Of course, you'd be responsible for the cookin' too. The helpers' quarters are close by, that's where you'd be livin'. You'll have your own privacy there. It's ready for you to move into, and you can fix it how you like. It's already furnished with basic necessities, if you need anything else, you can make a list and I'll try and fill it for ya. I'll need you to come daily to the main house to provide meals, clean and sew as needed. Some light paperwork and secretary things. The quarters aren't far from the main house, where I will be, and you can walk it easily. I have a surrey too that you could use to make trips back to visit your kinfolk if you wanted. You'd be off holidays, half day Saturdays, and if you go to church, all day on Sundays. You'll get free room and board, as well as a small monthly salary. I expect this to be for as long as needed. If you're lookin' for a temporary situation let me know because I can't use ya if that's your plan."

"It sounds fine to me. Mr. Anderson. I do have something I need to mention. I have a nine-year-old son that will be coming with me. He's a good boy and is a big help. He won't be any trouble or cause you any problems. I'm sorry, but if you don't want to give me the job because of my son I'll understand."

"I don't think that'll be a problem Mrs. Martin. The housekeeper that lived there before had two sons and a husband, so as long as he don't cause trouble, he's welcome too. I'd be proud for you to take the job. Was that your son that came to the door?"

"Yes sir. I hope he was polite to you."

"He seemed fine. Just you and the boy? Not getting personal mam but no husband?"

"No, it's just us. I'm a widow."

"I'm sorry to hear that mam. Well not to be too rude but how soon could ya start?"

"I can start as soon as you need me, Mr. Anderson."

"Well, I don't plan on comin' back to town again for another month or so. Could you start today? I can let you and your son ride with me in the buckboard back to the ranch. I have room in the back, I'll gettin' a few extra supplies since you and the boy will need it."

"I don't' have a lot of things sir. But can you give me a little bit of time to freshen up and collect my boy? If you come back in an hour, we should be ready."

"That works for me. If there is anything I can get for ya before we leave just write it down and I'll work on collectin' it while you're gettin' ready."

"I don't think I need anything Mr. Anderson. I do have one more question. My boy, Jacob, is in school here in Nightshade, and I'd like him to continue if possible. I know they will be out soon when spring is over so if he can finish up fine, but if not, I'd like him to start back after summer. He loves to go, and I'd hate for him to have to give it up if it's possible."

"The Lowoods family down the road from the Triple S, have a daughter about his age. She goes to school sometimes. He could go with her if you don't mind. I'm sure Mrs. Lowoods would be fine with it. She only lets little Gennie go to school when one of her boys can be off the farm to ride with her. Gennie could drive them, and he ride along. Might talk to her about it when we get back. Would that be good for ya?"

"Well, I think he could do that, if Gennie wouldn't mind him going. I think that might be just fine."

"I'll see you in an hour then."

"Thank you, Mr. Anderson. I really look forward to working for you."

# CHAPTER 18

Hannah went to find Naomi to tell her about taking the job with Mr. Anderson. She was happy that now everything was falling into place. She and Jacob would have their own house, well their own, and it didn't bother her that the man she would be working for wasn't half bad looking. He did seem a little sad. Maybe that was what Mr. Grover was talking about. She knew enough about living alone to recognize that kind of sadness. It wasn't grief. Grief is a different thing than sadness. Grief is a whole-body emotion. Not like sadness. Being sad is an emotion of the heart. When you're sad you can still function day by day. Grief is something that takes on the whole body. It leaves you lost and hopeless. Hannah was familiar with them both. She grieved a long time over Jack. It took a while to get over him, but she had to think of her son's well-being now. The Lord knew her pain. He made a way for them. Now, there were less of the sad days and very few of the grieving days. Now she had hope. It came in the form of a tall, rugged cowboy and a thing called the Triple S.

# CHAPTER 19

Naomi was glad for Hannah to be on her own again. She had a feeling about that cowboy. She had heard a few rumors in town about him. Really just gossip, was all. How he wasn't very personable and rarely spoke unless spoken to. She couldn't really blame him, since she and Robert had moved to town, it didn't take long to figure out who you could trust with information and who you couldn't. The postmaster for one seemed to know a little more than he should about Hannah coming to town before she even arrived. When Naomi sent for her in a postcard, she thought she saw him reading more than just the address. It was cheaper to send a postcard than a regular letter. From then on, she decided that paying the price for a regular letter would be worth the money in order to be discreet. She tried to stay away from the nosey ladies in town, but it was hard to dodge them most of the time. And invariably she was trapped in uncomfortable conversations about the goings on in Nightshade. Sam had been the topic of conversation one day while she was at the general store doing some shopping. There was a small group of ladies, speaking in veiled whispers but none too loudly. It was enough for Naomi to discern that the tall, sad cowboy was the topic of the day. It was said that he had been a long-lived bachelor after being jilted at the altar by his fiancé. Folks said he was never the same after that. Now Hannah was going to work for him as his housekeeper. Naomi figured it wouldn't be long before the gossip club would have additional subjects to spice up the conversations. He seemed pleasant enough to her when she met him at the door today.

But more than anything it could be good for Hannah and Jacob. They both would have their own home and if any trouble came around, this man seemed the type to take care of it. And too, she could still see Hannah every so often when she came back to town. Seemed to be the perfect match, as far as she could see.

Hannah sat down with Jacob to tell him about moving out to the Triple S. She answered all his questions about where they would live, school and what her job would be working for Mr. Anderson.

"Will we come back to see Ms. Naomi sometimes," he asked

"Well, yes, I'm sure we will need to come to town sometimes to get supplies. We may be able to see her too some Sundays at church. We will just have to figure that out with Mr. Anderson first, but I think he wouldn't mind too much. School will be something we will work on with one of the families that live near Mr. Anderson. They have a daughter that goes occasionally so I bet you can hitch a ride together."

"Ok mama. If you think it's good, then I think it's good."

"We have to get our things together. Mr. Anderson will come back for us in a little while, so I'll help you put together everything you want to bring."

Sam was moving supplies around in the buckboard to make room for Mrs. Martin and her son's belongings thinking about what he was getting himself into. Well, he guessed it could have been worse. He could still be lookin' for a housekeeper if Mrs. Martin hadn't answered the want ad. The pickens were slim to none from this little town. But he had to admit she seemed smart, healthy. She was pretty. He figured he got a fair deal. They would have to work out some minor details, but that shouldn't be hard to sort out. Sam stopped back in at the Editor, after getting supplies; and told Grover he wouldn't need another month on the ad. It was close enough to an hour, so he made his way over to the house to see if she and the boy were ready. They should make it home before dark.

Naomi answered the door this time, seeing the familiar handsome face of the tall cowboy standing in front of her. She invited him in. Sam tipped his hat with a nod and a thank you as he stepped inside the doorway. Hannah was waiting with Jacob in front of the staircase. She had two small leather valises beside her and was holding a little black pocketbook with one hand, holding Jacob's hand with the other.

Hannah decided to wear her blue linen dress for the ride back with Sam. It was the best dress she had, and Naomi told her it brought out the blue in her eyes. She wore it a few times to the church socials and thought it would be a nice look to start out in her new job. Instead of her hair down she pulled it back with a velvet ribbon, thinking it would be easier to manage on the drive out to the ranch. Jacob looked up at her and said, "You look pretty mama."

"Thank you honey. I want you to meet Mr. Anderson. We're going to be living on his ranch and I'll be working for him now. Mr. Anderson, this is Jacob, he is the man in my life."

Sam held his hand out to Jacob. Jacob hesitated a minute, but Hannah nudged him to return the offer.

"You can shake his hand Jacob, that's how gentlemen greet each other." Jacob slowly let go of Hannah's hand and gave Sam a loose handshake.

"Well nice to meet you, can I call you Jacob?"

"Yes sir. Are you taking us to your ranch?"

"That's the plan Jacob. As long as your mother agrees to it".

"Mr. Anderson was nice enough to let us ride back with him in his wagon Jacob. Go ahead and thank him."

"Thank you Mr. Anderson."

"Your welcome son."

"I'll get your bags then. If you'll just follow me." Sam wished Naomi well while Hannah and Jacob, both hugged her and kissed her goodbye. Then he scooped up the two valises and made his way out the door to the buckboard with Hannah and Jacob following behind. She didn't have much in the way of luggage, he thought, maybe it was because she didn't feel comfortable about taking up space in the buckboard. Either way he assumed she had what she needed so he set the bags underneath his seat in the bottom of the wagon. Sam lifted Jacob up with his long-muscled arms sitting him down in the middle of the seat, then turning to Hannah, offering her his hand and helping her to step up into the wagon. He climbed up in the driver seat, gripped the reins and clicked to the horses to 'get up.' Off they went with Hannah only looking back once to give a final wave to Naomi. All three-sitting side by side, eyes forward, looking ahead towards a strange and curious new life.

# CHAPTER 20

There was very little talking being done on the ride to the Triple S. Sam wasn't too much for small talk and Hannah wasn't sure what to say. Jacob on the other hand had no trouble prattling on about farm animals and such. He wanted to know how many cows Sam had, could he pet one, could he milk one, did he ride his horses much, could he ride one, did Sam have a dog, were there rabbits and squirrels to hunt, would he have his own room and his own bed, when could he start back to school, were there any kids around? Sam a little, overwhelmed, felt like he was back in the middle of the Lowoods boys with Jacob as the role of little Gennie. He only gave yes and no answers to Jacob, adding little to encourage a conversation. That Jacob was a smart little thing. Chatty but smart. He seemed to want to know everything he could about ranch life. Sam tried to remember if he was like that as a kid. What a handful for his mother if that were true. He wondered if Hannah felt that way at times. Taking care of a growing little boy on your own couldn't be easy. She didn't say anything much about her husband. He knew Tom had helped Serita with the boys often, but she was the one that did most of the raisin'. He watched Tom many a time send the boys her way when they needed discipling. Tom just didn't have the heart to scold them. Serita had no problem. Sam had seen her pop them with a dish rag plenty of times for fighting with each other. Boys do that from time to time. They respected her though. It didn't take much for them to fall in place when their mama took to them.

Tom just would wag his head and say, "them boys are full of wild weeds and thistle." Only once did Sam see Tom correct them. That was when Allen had sassed Serita about having to help with house chores. Tom spun him around by his collar and made him apologize to his mother. The look of surprise on Allen's face was too funny at the time and Sam had tried hard not to laugh. He never heard Allen say a cross word to his mother again after that.

Far as he could tell Jacob was a good boy. Of course, he had no kids of his own to compare but he had been around enough of them to believe he could make a fair judgement of it. Hannah seemed to him to be a kindhearted woman. She still wore her wedding ring. He noticed it when he squeezed her hand today. He wondered about her husband, what kind of father or husband he was. Sam didn't want to be too personal to ask her about it. He figured the townsfolk likely knew her story. He really shouldn't be wondering about her at all. Being so close and tied in with Dalton's lives these past years made him think it wasn't proper to barge into Hannah's personal history. He came to think of the Daltons as family. This woman wasn't family just the new housekeeper.

Hannah tried to imagine this as an adventure, much like the time she left home to marry Jack. It was a happy adventure then. Although this was an adventure, she wasn't sure about the happy part yet. She pictured the Triple S to be a plain and barren land, of dust and cows. Trying to figure out how she and Mr. Anderson fit in the picture was still hazy. Oh, she was grateful to Mr. Anderson for the job, but she didn't really know much about him. Grover Chambers told her a little. Anyway, how much can you really know someone from the things an old newspaper man said. He was nice so far. Naomi told her the story about the failed engagement as informed by the Nightshade gossip club. She couldn't imagine what would make a woman wait until a few days before her wedding to end a relationship. Maybe she didn't like his toughness and wanted a more sensitive, emotional man. Some women need that. Jack had been that way with her in the beginning. She had to admit it was attractive. But that faded with time. To tell the truth, she would have settled for a tough guy in the end to stand with her during the rough times. That was the past. Long gone. As long as Mr. Anderson kept her and her son safe and provided a roof over their heads, she wouldn't give it any more thought.

# CHAPTER 21

The wagon pulled up to the Triple S just before sundown. It had been a long trip. Jacob fell asleep on Sam's arm on the way home. Just like he had done so many times years ago. The boy had finally given out after all his three hundred and fifty questions, slowly crumbling into a little heap curled up between Hannah and Sam. It was still daylight when they arrived. The sunset was a particularly beautiful one. As they drove up to the helpers' quarters, Hannah was taken in by the vastness of the ranch. Sam told her it was eight hundred acres, but it seemed like twice that much. The pastures were all fenced with cows lined up along them. And the fences seemed to go on forever. There was a large pond where heifers and their calves were drinking. Some close to their mothers, some bunched together in groups of three or four. In the distance she could see what looked like a large brown barn. It had several doors in what Hannah assumed to be stalls. Just past the barn was another fenced pasture that had a dozen or so horses. She was sure she hadn't seen everything. From just where she was sitting, she was only able to look at a small portion of pasture at eye level. It was all so beautiful in the light of sunset. It reminded her of a pen and ink drawing she once saw in a magazine. Almost too real to believe. Maybe she would ask Mr. Anderson to take her on a tour of the property sometime. It certainly wasn't like the mountains of West Virginia.

She grew up in the valley of the Blue Ridge Mountains alongside her brothers and sisters. Living in the valley was the only life outside of Virginia that she knew, until her move to Arkansas. Her father was a coal miner, though he didn't make a lot of money, it was enough to make do. They never went hungry. They had two apple trees which resulted in pies, cobblers and dumplings. There was usually a hog killed every winter, salted and hung by strips in the smokehouse. A few chickens gave them eggs and meat. There were goats for milk or meat. In the spring, a garden with turnips, carrots and peas.

Hannah lived in a modest cabin with her parents, brothers and sisters. By mountain standards it was a fair size home. She shared a room with her oldest and younger sister. The brothers bunked up by twos in one bedroom and her parents had their own room. The nearest were ten miles away. Most folks living around or on the mountain were coal workers. The poorest families lived on the mountain while the lower middle-income families, like Hannah's, lived in the valley. They were a close-knit community, supporting one another through births, weddings and funerals.

The merchants in the valley provided the miners with food, equipment, clothing and pack animals. The only working ranches Hannah had known of were outside the valley in the plains. While she lived in Nightshade, it was all markets, buildings and stores much like the valley in West Virginia. Same wooden sidewalks, same saloons, same hurried people, same busy life. She thought it had to be different on the Triple S. How could it not be?

Sam pulled the wagon up to the helpers' quarters and gently woke Jacob up to let him see his new home. He rubbed his eyes and squinted to get a better look at the house. "Is this our home now, Mama?"

Hannah turned to Sam. "Well, Mr. Anderson, I'm assuming this where we will be staying."

Sam answered Jacob for her, "Yep, this is it son."

"Mrs. Martin the house is already stocked with food and essentials. If you need anythin' else just let me know. My housekeeper Serita left a few bed linens and kitchen utensils. There's a wood stove in the kitchen, a fireplace in the parlor and a small fireplace in the main bedroom. I'll make sure you have enough kindlin' when winter comes. But there should be plenty for what you'll be needin'. The house on the hill we passed up the road there is where I stay. I'll just set your things on the porch here with the supplies and you can sort em out where you want em later."

"That'll be fine Mr. Anderson. It's a lovely house. We shouldn't need anything but if I do, I'll be sure to tell you. "Would you show me around the house?" I know Jacob is going to love having his own room; Aren't you Jacob?"

"I never had my own room before." It's gonna be good here, right mama?"

Sam hesitated before answering Mrs. Martin request to give her a tour of the house. The last and only time, since Amelia, he had been inside was a year ago when Tom died. He wasn't planning on having too again now.

"Well mam, I really should be gettin' back up to the main house. It's getting' late. I'm sure you'll be able to find your way around without me buttin' in the way. The two bedrooms are at the back of the house, the boy might like the biggest one, it'll be next to the main bedroom where I expect you'll be sleepin'." Sam wanted to steer her away from the smaller bedroom where Jack had died. Not that it would have made much of a difference, people died at home all the time. But Sam didn't want to think about the last picture of Tom, now some stranger takin' in the same bed he'd passed away in.

"There's the root cellar with some raw vegetables, and if you walk that path there, there's a spring cellar with butter and milk just a few steps away. Outside the back of the house is a chicken coop. There are a couple of layin' hens that will give you eggs for cookin' if you like. But you'll need to let 'em out in the daytime to eat and close 'em up at night to keep 'em safe. You can see the well here in front. You just use the pump handle here and you'll get cold water."

"Same as the pump in the sink. Theres two jerseys that wander around the place, they'll come up a few times in the day to be milked. They're real gentle. I think you'll be able to find your way around everything. "I best be makin' my way on home now mam."

Hannah thought she saw him shuffle his feet a little and he lowered his head while he was talking about the house. He seemed smaller for some reason. She wondered if he was still haunted by some ghost, his friend, or maybe his girl? She decided she wouldn't push the subject and make do with exploring the house herself. Maybe there was more to this Sam Anderson than just rugged cowboy looks. There seemed to be a lot of knots twisted up in that man.

"Oh, and mam, before I leave you may be a needin' this." He climbed down from the surrey and pulled out one of the Colt pistols he usually carried with him. "When summer rolls around, we have a few issues with rattlesnakes comin' out to sun. You might see one in the chicken coop sometime. I suggest you keep this loaded for situations such as that, among other things. Just try not to shoot in my direction."

"Other things? Well, I hope not to have to use it but thanks for the offer. I guess I'll try and do some target shooting to get the feel of it."

"Hope to see you in the mornin' mam" and with that he tipped his hat, and climbed back into the wagon, clicking to the team of mules as they ambled up the road towards the main house.

# CHAPTER 22

Hannah and Jacob spent the rest of the evening in their new home, unpacking what little items she had packed and arranging them to each room as purposed. She helped Jacob put his things in the largest guest room where and how he wanted. Just a few dresses and nightclothes of Hannah's went into the main bedroom closet and night dresser. She pulled out the cotton nightgown from the dresser and slipped it over her head. The room was cozy with a small fireplace and dark blue curtains on the windows. The bed was covered in a matching quilt and pillows. A large flannel blanket was piled up in a roll at the end of the bed. She might need that when winter came along. She imagined lying in bed with a good book, a warm fire and the blanket wrapped around her for comfort. She sat on the edge of the bed and bounced on it a little to see how springy it was. Not bad. It wasn't as nice as the bed she and Jacob slept in at Naomi's, but it was ten times better than the one she had when she was married to Jack. The couple that occupied the bed before must have loved cuddling up with a fire together. Shame she hadn't had that opportunity in a long time. She missed Jack, as bad as he had been a husband or father, there was a time that she had felt different about him. She had loved the times when they had been close. A little tinge of warmness filled her face. In the early times of their marriage when he was sober, it had been a wonderful feeling. That was so long ago. She was thankful she had those memories to keep in her heart.

Hannah went in to kiss Jacob goodnight. Mr. Anderson was right. Having his room so close to hers made it easier to keep an ear and eye out on him. He was already asleep, half in and half out of his bed. Still had his traveling clothes on from the day, she gathered up his legs, swung them slowly over into his bed, pulled up the blanket over him and kissed him on the forehead. It had been quite a day for them both. She would make him change into clean clothes in the morning. Better to leave him in his old ones for now. She blew out the lamp and headed back to her room with the light of the moon guiding her to it. She would sleep well tonight. Tomorrow she would make breakfast then head up to the main house to cook for Mr. Anderson. For now, she would only dream about what the future could be for her and the little boy sleeping so soundly in bed. Her prayers for the night ended with thank you Lord for this thy blessing.

# CHAPTER 23

It seemed like she just had laid her head on the pillow when she opened her eyes. At first, she didn't know where she was. This wasn't Naomi's house, or bed. Slowly, it came back to her. She was at Mr. Anderson's ranch. It must be just before dawn. The sun had not even broken the clouds yet, but it was peeking light across the sky. She had to get up. Hannah picked her shawl out of the night dresser and put on her flat shoes from the closet. She made her way to the kitchen and lit the cookstove. It was late spring and still a little chilly in the morning before the sun came out. Hannah went outside and walked around to the back of the house. She found the root cellar filled with onions, carrots, turnips and potatoes. She gathered a few potatoes and onions and put them in the pockets of her gown. Then she walked the path to the spring cellar. It was a small stone building built right over a little brook, which rippled through a trench that flowed under the stone floor. There were a few shelves of butter and there was a covered stone jug of milk along with a few empty ones. It was cold inside, Hannah pulled her shawl around her and brought out a jar of butter and the milk. Sam must have milked the cows for her and put up a jug for today. She tasted it and was surprised at how creamy and wonderful it was. She walked back up the path to the house with her treasures thinking about cooking her first breakfast in the new surroundings. She woke Jacob up when she got back to the house. He was a hard sleeper. She had to shake him a few times before he was somewhat awake Rubbing his eyes he said. "I'm still sleepy mama."

"I know Jacob, but we've got a lot to do this morning and you need to get going. I'm gonna need you to go and get the eggs from the chicken coop and bring them in so I can make our breakfast. Now change into clean clothes and get going boy."

Jacob sat up, stretched his arms up high and slowly changed into a flannel shirt and a pair of blue overalls. He walked past Hannah in the kitchen, she was searching for pots and pans in the cabinets. He noticed his stomach was growling a little. Breakfast couldn't come soon enough. The chickens were scratching around in the dirt when he walked into the coop. There were five brown eggs nestled together in one nesting box. Jacob scooped them up in his hands and brought them to Hannah. "Look mama, aren't they something?"

"Yes, they are. You are going to be responsible for collecting the eggs in the morning and letting the hens out then making sure they're back in their coop in the evening. You think you can do that?"

"Oh sure. It will be fun. When will breakfast be done?"

"I'll call you when it's ready, you go let the hens out and clean out their nesting boxes, then come on back, should be done by then."

Jacob ran out, slamming the screen door behind him. Hannah just smiled to herself. He was growing up so fast. She didn't know if she was ready for that or not. Well, no time for squandering, better get back to breakfast.

# CHAPTER 24

She changed from her nightgown into a yellow print dress. It was one of her favorites and Jack had told her she looked like a pretty sunflower when she wore it. Jacob was ready and anxious to go see Mr. Anderson at his house. She put her hair back in a bun pulling tightly to the nape of her neck. Checking herself once again in the dresser mirror, she called Jacob to come. They walked the dirt road from their house up to the main house, and to Mr. Anderson. It was dawn now. The sun was full out and shining brightly through a maze of blue skies. It was going to be a perfect day. She held Jacob's hand talking about what life on a ranch may look like and how nice it was to be on their own in a house of their own. Well not really their own but she would describe it that way in their private conversations. When they arrived at the house, Hannah was amazed. It was so beautiful, and it looked bigger than when they drove past it yesterday. It had a giant porch with huge stately marble columns. The concrete steps up to the front door were long and tall. It took her a minute to take it all in. She knocked on the door, expecting a butler to open and usher her and Jacob inside. But instead, Sam opened it, standing there with a steaming cup of coffee and his hair tousled like she had seen Jacob's earlier that morning. He smiled and welcomed her and Jacob inside. Hannah thought how handsome he looked standing there.

"Please come inside. So how was your first night Mrs. Martin? Did you find your way around the place?"

"Yes, I did. I found a jug of fresh milk in the spring cellar. Did you leave it?"

"I did, those cows have to be milked every day or they'll run up dry. No more milk. I been doin' that since Tom couldn't anymore with his sickness. But now that'll be up to you or the boy every day."

"If you'll follow me, I'll show you where you'll be workin."

Sam led her, with Jacob following behind into the front parlor. There was a large multicolored rug underneath a brown cloth sofa. Three claw foot chairs, and a high back rocking chair. The windows were covered with white tapestry and lace. two corner tables, with kerosene lamps sitting on them. A wood mirrored bureau held a few books, portraits and a small ornate vase. She saw a large stone fireplace with an iron mantel in the corner. Hannah could picture, Sam's mother and father siting in this room, reading a newspaper, and sewing needlework napkins with a roaring fire to keep them warm.

"I don't spend much time in here, only just the few times Alvin and Star visited or Tom and Serita. Next is the linen closet," Sam made his way out of the parlor to a small door in the hallway.

"You'll find bed linens, towels, wash cloths and extra window coverings. If you need to change out those things they'll be here in this closet."

He pointed out the next room on the floor level." Library's in there and over there is a storage room." He walked to a room with large sacks printed with flour, corn meal, salt, sugar and canned goods that Serita put up before she left. Hannah saw jars of all kinds of figs, pears, apples, plums, peaches, jams and jellies.

"If you run low on anything in there, put it on a list for the month's supplies. Moving on to the next room."

"This is the dining room; I usually eat my breakfast in the kitchen. At supper and dinner I eat in the dining room. Breakfast around six a.m. as you likely figured, supper at one and dinner at eight." Hannah saw a large dining table that was surrounded by eight chairs with a laced tablecloth covering it. She wondered if Sam ate by himself since the housekeeper was gone, as he hadn't mentioned having many visitors.

"Upstairs are the bedrooms with closets in each. My room is the farthest down the end of the hallway. There are six bedrooms. Likely they won't need much tendin' to, since I'm the only one been livin' here."

He walked past Hannah and Jacob, "here is the kitchen, there's the cook stove, a pantry, pie saver, and buffet. You'll find dish wares in the cupboards, silverware in the buffet, and cookware under the sink. You can look everything over after breakfast to get yourself familiar with where things are. There are four fireplaces, the one in the parlor, in the library, and, one in my room, the fireplace in the guest bedroom is at the top of the stairs. Tell me when the wood stack is gettin' low and I'll bring some in from the woodshed during the cold weather. This old house keeps fairly warm when all the fires are lit. Serita kept the kerosene outside in a coal oil barrel. I have a few hens out back there, they keep me eggs for breakfast, Serita kept a few for cookin'."

Jacob filled Sam in on his new job on collecting the eggs and caring for the hens every day.

"That's a mighty important job boy."

Hannah was eager to get breakfast started, "Mr. Anderson, do I need to gather up anything to get breakfast going?"

I already have eggs set out; hens laid five fresh eggs this mornin'. There's a jug of milk on the table, and a loaf of bread ready for cutting' in the cupboard. it's wrapped in cheesecloth. Star sent me a loaf yesterday expectin' your arrival. You may need to bring milk with you tomorrow mornin' so's its fresh. I don't drink it that much, just mostly at night before bed. Coffee is my main drink and cold water. I'll eat just about anything you put before me; it's been a while since I've had a good meal. I'm lookin' forward to your cookin mam."

Hannah saw an apron sitting on the pump handle over the sink. She wrapped it around her waist and pumped a little water in her hands to freshen up. There was a coffee pot on the cookstove where, she assumed, Sam had gotten the coffee she saw him drinking at the door.

"I'm goin' out to check the fences mam. I should be back in time to eat breakfast."

"Can I go with you Mr. Anderson? I could help you." Jacob saw his chance to pet a cow or ride a horse.

"Fine with me, but you better check with your ma about that."

Hannah thought a minute. She really didn't need him hanging around the kitchen. Yes, that might be good for him to see how men work.

"Okay. But don't get in Mr. Anderson's way. He has important things to do. And don't you bug him about riding a horse. You're still too little for that right now. And try not to get too dirty."

Sam set his coffee on the table and motioned for Jacob to follow him. He grabbed his hat from the coat rack and off they went together, side by side out the front door.

# CHAPTER 25

Jacob stood in the barn amazed of how big it was. There were twelve stalls, five horses were in the barn, the other seven were out in the pasture. The mules were in a smaller pasture just outside of the barnyard. Sam gathered up his saddle, blanket and bridle from the tack room. He told Jacob to pick out one of the horses for him. Jacob stood back with his hands on his hips to survey each stall. He finally settled on a black mare with a spotted mane and tail. "How about this one Mr. Anderson? Can I lead her out".

"You ever been around a horse son?"

"Just at Naomi's house. My Uncle Robert has a walking horse that makes funny noises when he runs. I got to brush it once when Mr. Robert let me. My father never was around horses; he was always working at sea on a ship."

Sam took off his hat and scratched his head. He remembered a time when he was a kid, and his father had let him brush out, saddle, and ride his first horse. He remembered how good it felt to be near his father, being allowed to do those things on his own. He had watched Tom, and the boys work together while they were growing up. It was a humbling experience to now be in a position that called for him to be a mentor for a boy's first ride.

"All right. I'm gonna be right here to help you out. You have to demand respect from a horse. They weigh over 1000 lbs., which is over ten times what you're weighin' right now. As long as you show courage, they won't hurt ya, but show yourself to be weak, you're gonna have a problem there Jacob. Ya think you can do that?"

"I want to try. I've been wanting to ever since we got to Ms. Naomi's house, but Uncle Robert always told me I wasn't big enough yet. Am I big enough now you think, Mr. Anderson?"

"I wasn't much bigger than you are now son when I started messin' with horses. I think if you want to try bad enough it'll be ok. What should we tell your mom though?"

"I think we just wait a little bit on that, if its ok sir, she might worry some and I sure don't want to get on her wrong side. It can be something we tell her together once you think it's the right time."

Sam thought a second before he answered, "I think I'd agree with that. Bring that horse on out here boy and tie her to the hitchin' post."

Sam handed Jacob the lead rope and stood back to see how Jacob would take to handling a horse.

"What's her name, Mr. Anderson?"

"That's Sable, just pet her on the nose and show her your rope, she'll step right up to ya."

Jacob walked up to the stall door and held up the lead rope. Sure, enough, Sable walked right up to him and nickered softly. She lowered her head and Jacob patted her on the nose placing the open end around her neck with one end, holding the other end in his hand. He opened the stall door. Sable walked calmly behind him, head down, nuzzling him a little on his head when he stopped at the hitching post. Jacob tied the end of the lead rope around her neck and to the post. He smiled a proud smile as if he had just won a pot of gold.

"Fine job their son. Now let's brush her out, then we'll tack her up and you can ride double behind me. You watch how I saddle her and the next time you're here I'll let you put the blanket on. We'll just ride the south pasture this mornin' before we head back to the house for breakfast."

"Thanks, Mr. Anderson. I sure appreciate you sir."

Sam patted Jacob on the head, but he tried not to show too much emotion. There was a little moment of pride there. This boy wasn't afraid of a thing. You don't find that much with kids who weren't raised up on a ranch. Could be a big help to him not to mention he wasn't bad company. He finished saddling up the mare, pulled Jacob up by the arm and swung him behind him in the saddle. He took his time riding the fence line. Walking the horse along the edges of the pasture then back again. Jacob went on talking about how when he got bigger, he was going to have horses and cows and chickens and a dog. Sam listened with one ear on Jacob but kept his eyes on the fence row. Occasionally he would mutter a yes or no, or just nod to Jacob.

They finished up leading Sable back to her stall then putting fresh hay out for the other horses. Sam and Jacob walked back to the house for breakfast. Hannah already had the table laid out with scrambled eggs, butter, bacon and milk. She found a carton of flour and mixed up a pan of biscuits. She was just pulling the biscuits out of the stove when Sam and Jacob came in. Sam pulled off his hat and washed his hands and face before sitting at the table. He watched intently as Hannah dumped out the biscuits on an empty plate in front of him. "Looks and smells good Mrs. Martin. I'm awfully hungry this mornin."

"I hope Jacob didn't get in your way much Mr. Anderson. He can be a handful sometimes."

Sam winked at Jacob, "Oh no, he got a gift for talkin' though, but we made it without too many hiccups."

"I'm still full from breakfast at home mama, but can I have a biscuit? I wanna put some butter on it while its hot."

"Where are you putting everything child? Am I gonna have to get you some bigger pants now? Go wash your hands in the sink and I'll set you up for a biscuit with butter."

"Um, Mr. Anderson, I hope you don't mind but we always say grace before meals. I hope you're a praying man."

"Now Mrs. Martin, if you're tellin' me you require prayer before I eat your cookin' I'm gonna be a little worried about what you're puttin' on my plate."

"Please don't get sassy with me Mr. Anderson. If you want me to cook for you then we gotta be thankful for the food the good Lord is providing. So, if you don't want to say prayer that's fine, but for me and Jacob, there will be a blessing said here this morning. Just make up your mind what's it gonna be."

Sam could see that it was gonna be a contentious issue with this woman. He wasn't gonna like it much if she was already startin' out bossy. He only let Serita boss him because she earned that right over time. This was the woman's first day on the ranch and here she was already getting' up in his craw.

"See here Mrs. Martin, I ain't a saint but I ain't no heathen neither. I've been eatin' my breakfast without a prayer for over twenty years. I don't see how that needs to change now. But if you're leavin' me the choice of breakfast or no breakfast, then you go right ahead with your prayin', I'll just sit back and wait till you're done."

"All I ask is you bow your head during the blessing Mr. Anderson. You don't have to say a word. The Lord will accept it for the both of us. Now you bow your head please." Jacob bowed his head, but he peaked out of one eye to see if Sam Anderson was going to concede to his mother.

Sam didn't put up a fight. He bowed his head, grumbling quietly to himself. But refused to close his eyes. She couldn't make him participate totally. Afterall there weren't no woman could force him to pray. He was gonna need to rethink this whole situation. For now, he complied as requested.

# CHAPTER 26

As Hannah cleaned up the kitchen, she was beginning to understand what Grover Chambers told her about him. She remembered him saying, what was it, stubborn as a Charleston mule? Yes, she had her first look at that mule at breakfast this morning.

She didn't know much about mules, but she knew enough that although stubborn, they could be intelligent and reasonable. Sam Anderson just needed a little encouragement to figure out being reasonable was a better way of doing things. She just needed a way to go about making him see it. He would be a much more pleasant person to work for in the long run. At least he didn't have a drinking problem and he wasn't burdened with a family to provide for.

Hannah finished up in the kitchen and found Sam in the library wearing a pair of wire rimmed reading glasses. Jacob was still in the kitchen washing up. Sam was sitting in one of the leather backed chairs, his face buried in a history book. He heard her come in but acted like he hadn't noticed, thinking she was going to bring up the fact he wasn't happy about praying over breakfast.

Sam looked up from the book over his reading glasses. "I was just readin' up on Napoleon Bonaparte. Did you know that as a child he was bullied for not bein' a Frenchman? Isn't it strange that he grew up to be one of France's great leaders?

"I didn't know about him being bullied. He was a great leader, but in the end, he wound up in exile alone and sad."

Hannah changed the subject, sensing that the subject of Napoleon was being used to insinuate she was a bully.

'Mr. Anderson, I'm working on the supply list. You can look over it to add to or subtract from it. If you have any clothes that need washing, please put them in the sink. Anything that needs ironed should be set apart from the regular. I plan to get to the upstairs bedrooms sometime this week. Is there anything else you need me to do before I get started? Jacob can hang out the clothes for drying or he can help you out with chores if you just say so."

"No need for me to look it over. I'll take care of it. I need to ride over to the Lowoods later to see if they need help puttin' up the hay from yesterday's cuttin.' I could talk to Star about lettin' little Gennie ride to school with Jacob on days she might be goin'. Star is Mrs. Lowoods, mam. Maybe you and the boy might go along too. Star can talk woman talk with you if ya like that. I know a woman needs a woman friend sometimes when you're livin' around men."

"Well, I think I'd like that Mr. Anderson. Just having a woman friend can be like finding a new dress that fits perfect. Makes you feel good all over. Not many men would understand that, but women do."

"You'd be right about that mam. I don't have knowledge about those things. I have a few shirts and denims that need washed. I'll get 'em and pile 'em up in the sink there for ya. I can't think of anything else right now. After supper we'll plan on a visit to the Lowoods so they can meet you. Then we ought to be back to the Triple S in time for dinner."

Jacob found Hannah and Sam in the library. He heard them talking about meeting the Lowoods. As he came into the library, he felt tension in the room. Was it something to do with him, he wondered. He guessed it was just the dust up at the breakfast table. His mother had always been adamant about prayers for meals and bedtime, and church on Sundays. He guessed Mr. Anderson wasn't used to that. Not sure why he would be so upset about it, after all it wasn't him that was praying. And he knew he wasn't because he saw him keep his eyes open when mama said grace.

Jacob was in awe of all the books in the library. Sam noticed him staring with his mouth open.

"You like to read boy?"

"I do Mr. Anderson. That's why I like school. We get to read books and learn about all kinds of things. I never saw this many books before though."

Hannah tried to rush him out of the library. "Jacob, go get a bucket for me from the kitchen. Don't bother Mr. Anderson right now."

"Oh, he's fine mam. He's welcome to any of the books in here. I spent a lot of time in this library myself growin' up. Lots of good stories in them. Jacob might learn somethin' from some of these books."

"Can I Mr. Anderson? Are you kidding about letting me read your books?"

"As long as your mother doesn't have work for you to do, you come get me and I'll show you which ones are the best to read. As a matter of fact," Sam stood up and walked over to one of the shelves, reaching up to the top and pulling out a copy of Gulliver's Travels. He handed it to Jacob. "Here, you try this one, it starts with a shipwreck, wasn't your father on a ship?"

"Yes, he was. Can I take it home with me to read?"

"Keep it long as ya need. Just bring it back when you're finished, and we'll see what other books might interest you." Sam handed Jacob the book, and he opened it starting with the first chapter title, A Voyage to Lilliput.

"Thanks Mr. Anderson. Mama, can I take it with me?"

"Later, right now you come help me by picking some of those blackberries I saw outside of the house. Then you can help me get started on cleaning the upstairs. After that should be about time for supper. Now come on, get going."

Jacob carried the book underarm as he went to fetch a bucket from the kitchen to pick blackberries.

"Thank you Mr. Anderson, you just became a hero to that little mop headed boy."

"No problem mam, he's a good boy. I'll go out and get the surrey ready. I'll be busy for a few hours in the barn unless you need me for anything. Do ya think you'll be done by supper?"

"Yes, as long as you don't have a lot of clothes that need washing. I'll finish it and get started with supper after that."

# CHAPTER 27

Sam pulled the surrey out to give it a look over. He hadn't used it since taking Serita to the train depot. The seats were a little dusty, so he pulled out his handkerchief and wiped it down dry. He pulled down the cloth canopy and adjusted it over the front carriage. He was thinking that Mrs. Martin could strike up a friendship with Star, that way they could keep each other company. Sam admired her spunk but there were some lines that shouldn't be crossed. And she crossed one of those this mornin'. He had to admit, it was a little annoying her bein' so pretty and all. Good looks could be a distraction, he knew that all too well. He wouldn't be makin that mistake again. The boy though, hadn't figured on likin' the boy so much.

Sam went to the barn to get out a horse. Sable had already been worked for the day, so he decided on Skip, a roan gelding. He spent most of his time cleaning all the tack with saddle soap and didn't realize it was getting close to supper time. Leading Skip out of the barn he walked him up to the surrey. Then he backed him in and tacked up the harness. After securing the harness he tied Skip to the hitching post and walked back up to the house to check if supper was ready. Skip would wait there hitched, ready to travel.

Hannah finished washing and hanging out laundry. Sam only had three or four shirts, two pair or denims, a pair of long johns and three handkerchiefs to wash. It didn't take her long to wash them and hang them out on the clothesline. She was done cleaning the upstairs while Jacob was picking blackberries. Jacob left his book on the kitchen table as he picked a large bucket full of ripe blackberries for Hannah. He proudly presented them to her with his purple stained smile.

"Why Jacob what's this on your face?"

"Well, I may've eaten a few," he confessed.

Hannah just laughed at him; he was too cute to scold. She took them from him and thought she'd just might have to try one for herself. She popped a large berry in her mouth. They were sweet and luscious. She understood why Jacob couldn't resist.

"You know son, these are the sweetest berries I've ever had. You run along now and wash up. Supper will be ready in a bit."

Hannah had everything ready by the time Sam got back. She fixed up a pot of stew, corn fritters and blackberry pie. There was a jug of cold water sitting on the table with clean plates, silverware and crystal drinking glasses. She found cloth embroidered napkins in a drawer underneath the cupboard. Hannah placed them neatly underneath the silverware and beside each China plate. By the looks of things, that hadn't seen a table anytime soon. She had everything in place when Sam walked into the dining room.

The table looked better than the Royal Inn restaurant he had eaten at once in Nightshade. He waited for Hannah to take a seat, but she stood back and motioned for him to take a seat as she pulled a chair out for him. He noticed she was still wearing her apron. She looked beautiful with that auburn red hair of hers pulled back in a bun. Wiping the flour off her face with the tail of her apron she poured him a glass of water from the ceramic jug. For a minute, just for a minute, he felt a little twinge in his stomach. Not lingering on the subject, he gratefully took his place at the table and pulled his chair up close. Hannah piled his plate with stew and corn fritters. Then, after serving Sam, she and Jacob sat down, and bowed her head. She waited for Sam to do the same.

Still reluctant, but not needing prodding, he bowed his head.

Jacob did the same. He still refused to close his eyes. He had to keep some dignity intact.

'Thank you, Lord, for this thy bounty, may you be blessed as you have blessed us with this food. Amen."

"Amen! Jacob shouted, let's eat!"

# CHAPTER 28

"Mighty fine supper there, Mrs. Martin. That blackberry pie was better than the restaurant at the Royal Inn Hotel in Nightshade. And the stew sure puts meat on a person's bone."

"Thank you, Mr. Anderson. I hope you didn't mind me using your fancy table napkins. It just seems to me a meal tastes better when you're surrounded by pretty things."

Sam wouldn't argue with that, but he wasn't thinking about fancy napkins bein' the pretty things.

"Well, I'm headed out to get the surrey ready. I'll drive up to the front and when you're ready, you and the boy just come on."

'I've only got a little bit left to put up in the kitchen. It won't take a minute. Jacob, could you go and help Mr. Anderson with the surrey?"

"Ok, mama, I will"

"Oh, and Mr. Anderson I hope it's all right, but I saved some of the blackberry pie for Mrs. Lowoods and her family."

"Well, that would be quite neighborly Mrs. Martin. There's a pie saver in the pie safe, you might use that to put it in. Just save me a little bit for breakfast in the mornin' if you would. It'd taste right fair with a cup of coffee before breakfast."

"I'll be happy to Mr. Anderson. I'll meet you both in a bit."

Sam and Jacob climbed up in the surrey. Jacob needed a little help, so Sam pulled him up by the arm and sat him down right beside him. He had to stop thinking about that red hair and those blue eyes. The picture of her in that apron wiping the flour from her face was giving him a sore headache. It had to be because he ate too much. She was as good as and better than Serita at cooking. Serita didn't use the fancy glasses and napkins. She just fixed everything to taste good, not so much as to look good. Not that he had any complaints about Serita or Hannah for that matter. This was just something different, he wasn't used to. Sam clucked to Skip to move on as he drove up to the front of the house.

Hannah came out holding the pie saver, wrapped up in a kitchen dish cloth. She handed it to Sam as his hand lightly touched hers during the exchange. He thought he saw her blush a little, likely due to the heat of the day, he supposed. He was busy thinking about it, not noticing she was already climbing up into the surrey by herself.

"I'm sorry Mrs. Martin, I should have come around to help you in."

"I'm not an invalid Mr. Anderson. Don't you worry about me, you just keep your attention that the pie saver isn't jostled around during the ride. I'd hate to present the Lowoods with a mush of blackberries on my first visit to them."

"Yes mam. Get up Skip."

# CHAPTER 29

Sam pulled the surrey up to the Lowoods and hitched Skip to a tree. He helped Jacob and Hannah out, then reached in and handed her the pie saver. This time being careful to refrain from any hand touching. The hound dogs, got up from the porch and began their howling to signify company arriving. Star opened the screen door and came out, shielding her eyes with her hand to keep the sun out, and to get a good look at who it was coming towards her. "That you Sam?"

"Yes mam, thought I'd bring my new housekeeper and her boy to visit with you."

"Who you got there with you Sam?"

As they got to the porch, where Star was standing, Sam reached out his hand to greet her.

"Star, I'd like you to meet Mrs. Hannah Martin, and this is her son Jacob."

"Hello, Mrs. Lowoods, I've heard some good things about you and your family."

"Well goodness Sam, looks like you picked a pretty one. Nice to meet you Mrs. Martin, good looking boy there too."

Sam saw her blush again, just like when their hands touched with the pie saver. He felt uncomfortable for Hannah, same as when the townsfolk asked him about Amelia.

"Well thank you Mrs. Lowoods. I'm afraid I wasn't prepared to meet you properly, or I would have been dressed better. Jacob can you tell Mrs. Lowoods it's nice to meet her."

Jacob kicked the dirt around, shoving his hands in the pocket of his overalls while giving a halfhearted "umm nice to meet ya".

"He's a little shy around strangers Mrs. Lowoods, you'll have to forgive him."

"Oh shush, I've got four boys of my own, I know how they are. He'll grow out of that soon enough, then you'll be wondering where time went. Come on in. Alvin and the boys are out in the hayloft, Sam. I think, Alvin wanted to see you if you want to go on. Me and Gennie will keep this boy and his mama occupied while you're gone."

"I'll be on my way then Star, Mrs. Martin will you be all right with me leavin' you with Star for a little bit. She's got a way about her when company's around."

"Oh, you just go on about your business Sam Anderson. We don't need the likes of you butting in where you aren't welcomed." Then in Iroquoian she called him a cranky old buzzard.

Sam walked out to the hayloft, laughing as he went.

Star held open the door while Hannah and Jacob went inside. The house was smaller than the helpers' quarters. She wondered how they managed with all those boys and a little girl. It was clean and tidy, not a bit of dust anywhere, no clutter not even a crumb laying around. Star lead them through the front room to a larger room with a sofa, a few chairs and a large bear skin rug on the wood floor. There was a well-worn Bible laying on top of the mantel and painted picture of what Hannah supposed to be Jesus. She and Jacob sat together side by side on the sofa. Star pulled up one of the chairs and sat in front of both of them.

"You'll have to ignore Sam, Mrs. Martin, he always tries to get me riled up, but I've caught onto his teasing ways. He's really a good man, he just needs a little polishing up in the manners department. I've known him for many years, and he hadn't changed a bit since the first time Alvin, and I met him. How did you come to be his housekeeper? I know he's been looking for someone to take Serita's place. Are you the one he told us about, from a month ago?"

"No, that was another lady He said he talked to her before

hiring me, it just didn't work out. Jacob and I rode out with Mr. Anderson, yesterday. We'll be staying in the helpers' quarters. I have a blackberry pie here. Would you like to save it for when your family is together at the next meal?" She handed the pie saver to Star.

"Oh my, thank you so much Mrs. Martin, we don't have many blackberries around the farm, this will go good with our dinner later tonight. It's awfully kind of you to think of us. Star took the saver and placed it on the table beside her chair. I'll put this in the kitchen later after we're done talking. By the way just call me Star, I think that's called for since we're almost neighbors."

"I'm Hannah. It'll be my pleasure Star. Sam told me you have a daughter that goes to school in Nightshade every so often. Is that right?"

Jacob was paying strict attention to this part of the conversation. He leaned in close to Hannah to see how this was going to go, the thing about school.

"Just a minute, Gennie? Gennie come here I want to introduce you to our new neighbors!"

From another room in the house, came a lanky little girl with long dark hair in a dress with a ruffled collar and hem. She was a beautiful girl, like Star, and she had the same dark eyes and long dark lashes.

"Gennie, this is Mrs. Martin, Sam's new housekeeper and her son Jacob."

"Hello Mrs. Martin, hello Jacob."

Jacob didn't know what to say. This girl wasn't like the girls at Ms. Naomi's house. She had nice eyes and freckles on her cheeks. For a girl she was, he didn't want to say cute, but she wasn't ugly.

He barely whispered a hello to Gennie. But he knew she heard him, because she smiled at him when he said it.

"Nice to meet you, Gennie. I heard that you go to school. Is there a favorite subject you're learning about?"

"Well, I like them all, but I think my favorite is reading. My mother taught me a lot of reading from the Bible, but I get to read different books at school. So, I'd say that was my favorite subject."

"That's Jacob's favorite too. He was going to Nightshade for school a few months, maybe you saw each other in class."

Star interjected "She hasn't been going much the past few months Hannah, we have to have the mules to work the crops, and I can't let her go by herself, so it's not likely she knew about your Jacob."

Hannah went on "I was wondering, maybe Jacob could ride with her to school. I know it's already time for school to be closed for the season, but come fall, they could go together if you would permit it."

"Hmm. I'll have to talk it over with Alvin first. It's a thought. Jacob, would you mind riding on an old farm mule with Gennie?"

"No mam. I 'd like that."

"Well, it's better than ridin' with an aggravatin' brother. As long as you don't tease me, or pinch my cheeks, I think I'd be allright about it."

Star wanted Gennie to get all of an education as she could. Alvin couldn't be against it. He would still have the boys for farm work and sparing one of the mules shouldn't be a problem. She would talk to him about it after dinner, once he had his fill of blackberry cobbler.

"All right, I'll take it up with your father later tonight. Gennie why don't you and Jacob go outside, you can show him the tree swing your brothers put up yesterday."

"Is it all right mama?"

"Yes son, just mind your manners."

Jacob and Gennie ran out the door, slamming the screen door behind them."

"I don't think there's a door in the county that hadn't been slammed shut by a kid in a hurry."

Hannah laughed, "I know what you mean, it's a rite of passage I guess."

"So, how's your first day working for Sam?"

"I think it went fine. We did get off to a bumpy start at breakfast this morning when I asked if we could say grace before our meal."

"Sam saying grace? That's like asking a hog to take a bath. He isn't much on praying or bible reading. Serita tried for years to get him to go to church with them, but he never set foot in the door, kind of like that with that house you're staying in."

"I thought he acted a little strange yesterday evening when I asked him to show me around the house. He acted like I was going to pull a tooth. I wondered if it had something to do with his fiancé or his friend dying there."

"I think both, Hannah. First off, he built that house for his Amelia when they were to be married. He and his father spent a lot of time and sweat on that place. Shame on her for doing that to the man. I didn't know him before her, but I can tell you, he is still walking around with a lot of hurt inside. I think it probably stirred up the devil in him when Tom died. Don't judge him for it. He needs someone to trust, he sure wouldn't think of asking the Lord to help him. But the Lord has ways of helping folks when they're not looking for it. Maybe you're the help he needs."

"Oh, I don't know. I thought that way when my husband was alive. I tried for years to help him, and it didn't turn out good. So, I wouldn't be so sure I'm one to help anybody. But I will say a prayer for Mr. Anderson tonight."

# CHAPTER 30

"Looks like you got enough hay to last for the winter Alvin." Sam jumped down from the loft ladder, landing on his feet in front of Alvin Lowoods.

"Yea, we don't have too much to feed this season, just a few mules, hogs and a milk cow. If we get lucky, winter will be a mild one again this year."

"Thanks for the hay, Mr. Anderson, when you get ready to drive the cattle in, we'll be ready."

"Appreciate that Matt. I'll be hittin' ya up around the end of September. I got a lot of good steers in this bunch, should bring good pay to you boys at auction."

"You boys go on, find your brothers and check on the mules, they need fresh water. Matt, you and James get the pitchfork and rake the hay straggles. We'll use that to put in the chicken boxes. Me and Sam are gonna take a walk around the wheat field. Come on Sam."

Sam followed Alvin out of the barn down a pathway which led out to the Lowoods wheat field. The wheat covered almost ten acres. Sam was surprised how thick it had grown.

"Looks like you got yourself a bumper crop there this year Alvin. I don't think I've ever seen a wheat field so full. You should get good prices for it."

Alvin reached down, pulled a blade of wheat, and put it in his mouth, chewing on the raw end.

"Gettin' that last rain, didn't hurt it none. We been blessed this year. Corn too. I'll have the boys fix you up with a tow sack so you can feed some of your stock. Or you can save some for that Mrs. Martin to cook up a mess for ya. By the way, speakin' of Mrs. Martin, I seen her when you pulled up, she's not hard to look at Sam, case you hadn't noticed."

"She's a fair lookin' woman, and no I hadn't made it a point to notice. I got to say, she knows her way around a cook stove. Serita would have approved of her, I think. Mrs. Martin fixed a fine breakfast and supper today. But she's a little pushy, and that puts a kink in my neck. She's gonna have to understand I have my own ways of doin' things. The boy is a bonus. He reminds me of myself at his age."

"Well Sam, maybe you're just set in your ways a little bit. She could be good for ya. A woman's way can sure make life easier on a man sometimes. It sure did me good when I met Star. Can't imagine what I'd be doin' if she hadn't come along."

"Star is different Alvin. I barely know this woman and she comes into my house tell'n me that I wouldn't be gettin' no breakfast unless a prayer was said first. Well, that it'n my way Alvin. I had enough badgerin' from Serita every Sunday for fifteen years. I'm not about to start in with Mrs. Martin."

"I hear ya. But she's not Serita and she's not Amelia, Sam. I wasn't much on Bible readin' or goin' to church before Star. Now, I kinda like the time we spend together doin' those things. Maybe the Lord got her mixed up with you for a reason, couldn't hurt anything if you just give it a try. I never knowed nobody that got hurt or died from just sayin' a little prayer."

"I don't have anything against those that participate Alvin, that's between you and the good Lord. As for myself I'm just tryin' to keep the ranch goin' and all my attention goes to that. Whatever else the Lord has on his mind, he can work it out between him and Mrs. Martin, I'm doin' just fine without it."

Alvin chuckled to himself. "Sounds like this woman is getting on more than just your nerves Sam".

Sam briskly turned walking away, muttering under his breath to Alvin. "That's enough about that Alvin. I think we oughta head back to the house. I gotta be getting' back to the Triple S. Day's a wastin'."

# CHAPTER 31

Sam and Alvin were almost back to the house when Jacob saw them coming in from the wheat field.

"Look Mr. Anderson, look how high I can push Gennie" Jacob gave the swing a big push, Gennie was standing up on the seat holding onto its ropes.

"Higher Jacob!" Gennie screamed, her dark hair flying in the wind.

Sam didn't acknowledge Jacob or Gennie he wasn't listening to them. He walked past them and made his way to the front porch. Sam opened the door, with Alvin following close behind. Both women, were deep in conversation, but upon hearing the door slam shut, they switched their attention to Alvin and Sam.

"You get all the hay up Alvin?" Star leaned forward in her chair as both men came into the room.

"Yep, Sam and the boys finished it up, the boys are workin' on gatherin' up the hay straggles now. They should be done in a bit."

"Mrs. Martin, I mean Hannah, brought us a homemade blackberry pie. I bet it'll taste good as it looks and smells."

Sam had a sour look on his face. Hannah didn't know what had upset him. It must have been something that happened between him and Mr. Lowoods.

"We need to get back to the Triple S, Mrs. Martin. I hate to interrupt your visit with Star but there's some things that need tendin' to."

"Of course, Mr. Anderson, I need to get back and get Jacob

cleaned up, thank you Star for letting us into your home. It's been so nice to meet you and your family. I hope we can meet again soon."

"Do you go to church anywhere Hannah? We are going this Sunday, if you'd like to go. Maybe Sam would let you take the surrey."

"Yes, I've been with my cousin Naomi to the church in Nightshade. I'd be obliged to go together with you if you don't mind is that all right with you Mr. Anderson?"

Sam was getting fidgety, he didn't want to be in the middle of any conversation that involved the words church, prayer, Serita or Amelia. Next thing you know, he'd be wrangled into goin' to church. Nope, not gonna happen. He nodded both to Star and Hannah.

"Fine, fine, let's go now Mrs. Martin, I'll get Jacob while you say your goodbyes."

And with that he turned on point, giving a halfhearted wave to Alvin and a curt thanks to Star for the visit. He walked back to the front door and out to roundup Jacob.

Star pulled Hannah aside and whispered to her, repeating that she was welcome to go to church with them Sunday if she still was interested.

"Nice to meet you Mr. Lowoods, I hope you all enjoy the pie, I'll get the pie saver Sunday if that's okay. Goodbye." Hannah assumed it was going to be a long ride back to the Triple S.

Sam was in such a hurry; he was almost rude. She didn't expect him to talk about what was bothering him. He sure was an obstinate man. Charleston mule, there it was again.

"Come on boy it's time to leave", Sam waved to Gennie then picked Jacob up, carrying him on his shoulders all the way to the surrey.

"Goodbye Gennie, thanks for the swing"

"Goodbye Jacob, see you again sometime."

Sam lifted Jacob off his shoulder and swung him over into the surrey. Hannah just behind them both, and without a hand from

Sam, lifted herself up sitting herself down on the seat, Jacob between them both.

"Get up Skip", Sam slapped the reins, and the horse took off with a little jump. He was muttering something Hannah couldn't understand.

"What did you say, Mr. Anderson?"

"I didn't say nothin', I just wish people would keep their noses out of my business. Present company included."

"I can't say I know what you're talking about, but I haven't been in your business Mr. Anderson."

"Mr. Anderson, Gennie likes to read just like me, can I loan her my book when I finish it, so she can read it too?"

Sam didn't hear what Jacob was asking, he was too busy thinking about Alvin Lowoods buttin' in his affairs. Alvin was a friend but that didn't give him the right to pass judgement. After all he had four boys to keep his farm goin', and no need for a housekeeper. He didn't need advice from someone that had no sense about dealin' with hired help.

"Get up Skip!" He smacked the reins again, and again Skip took a little hop, taking the surrey a little faster than before.

"If you don't mind, I'm not in that big a hurry to get back. Im sure the horse won't mind either."

"I'll be the one to decide that, unless you think you should pray about it."

Hannah decided it would be best to refrain from saying anything else. "I wouldn't bother Mr. Anderson about Gennie borrowing that book right now, Jacob, there will be plenty of time to discuss it before you see her again."

"Plenty of time," muttered Sam.

# CHAPTER 32

Sam stopped the surrey in front of the house, helping Jacob out and barely speaking to Hannah. She got out, not waving or saying goodbye to Sam. "I guess you'll be eating dinner on your own tonight, Breakfast in the morning then Mr. Anderson?"

"Fine, then". Off he took, Skip kicking up his heels, as the surrey went out of sight.

"What's the matter with Mr. Anderson mama? Is he mad about me asking to lend his book to Gennie?"

"No son, he's just tired from helping Mr. Lowoods put up hay. He'll feel better after a good night's sleep. Speaking of sleep, we need to milk the cows and get washed up for our own dinner before the nights over with."

"Can I help you milk mama?"

"Yes, let me wash my hands here and you help to call them in. There should be a pail in one of those sheds, can you find one for me and bring it out with you?"

"Ok mama." He headed out to the kitchen in search of a milk pail, while Hannah washed her hands at the well pump.

She met Jacob out on the porch, with the pail in his hand. "Well, I guess we better call them up Jacob. Here cow, here cow, come on in cow, here cow."

Just as soon as she called, up came two doe eyed heifers, both sauntering up the path. They stopped in front of Hannah and Jacob. Hannah patted them on the head. "I don't know what they call you two, but I think I'll just name you Butter and Biscuit. What do you think about that Jacob?"

"I like that. Here," he handed her the pail.

"Can you get me that stool off the porch there Jacob? I'll need it to milk."

Hannah hadn't milked any cows, only goats growing up in West Virginia, shouldn't be that much different with a grown cow. A cow was just a big goat.

It was the same, but it was way more milk than any of goats she ever milked. Hannah took the pail of milk from Butter and hauled it to the spring cellar and poured it into one of the empty jugs she saw earlier sitting on the shelf. After finishing up with Biscuit, she took the milk into the house, ready to be consumed with dinner. Nothing like a warm glass of milk after a long day.

"Let's get ready for dinner Jacob. Are you hungry?"

"Yes mam."

"Ok wash up your hands and face then."

Hannah fixed a meal of potatoes, turnips and beef. She hadn't realized she was so hungry, until the smell of food filled the kitchen. She and Jacob sat down to the table." Dear Lord, thank you for the food you have set before us this day. Thank you for the blessing of meeting new friends today. Please help Mr. Anderson have a better day tomorrow and give him rest in his heart. Amen"

"Does Mr. Anderson get tired in his heart too mama?"

"I think he is a little afraid to trust new people right now Jacob, you don't worry about it. Sometimes hearts get tired too. You're his friend. He just needs a little help with big people. Now eat your dinner." After dinner, Hannah sent Jacob out to round the hens up and put them back up in the coop for the night. When he got back in the house, Hannah could see he looked a little tired himself.

"Ok, I'll get your bath ready, then you go on to bed after you say your prayers. We are going to have another busy day tomorrow."

Hannah set up the wash tub for Jacob's bath. She poured a pot of boiling water from the teapot into the wash tub and cooled it with a pot of well water. Then she set out a bar of soap and clean towels. "Jacob your bath is ready now, come on."

"Here I am."

While he was bathing, she cleaned up the kitchen and set out clean clothes to wear for the morning.

"I'm done mama; I'm ready to put on my nightgown."

"It's on your bed Jacob, I think I'm going to wash up myself then I'm going to bed."

"Are we sayin' grace for breakfast at Mr. Anderson's house tomorrow?"

"You just don't worry about that now, go on, get dressed for bed."

"I'm gonna read about Gulliver before I go to sleep."

"Don't stay awake too, long son. I love you, don't forget to say your prayers."

"Love you too mama. I'm gonna pray for Mr. Anderson and his tired heart."

Hannah knew tomorrow would be another test of patience. She could only hope for a good night's sleep to be ready for battle with Mr. Sam Anderson. Lord knows she was going to need it.

# CHAPTER 33

Sam didn't think he was being too unreasonable. He got home from the Lowoods, still smoldering about the whole thing. Hannah was his housekeeper, not a wife that was the difference. For all purposes she was still a stranger. True, she was fair to look at, especially when she blushed. And she was a spirited thing, not that it was bad, but it didn't suit his situation very well. He was thinking to himself about these things, while raking sawdust in the barn. Skip was in his stall grazing on the corn Alvin sent home. Well, he'd apologize to Alvin, in the next day or so. He hadn't meant to be short; he just couldn't understand what made people so intent on thinkin' they knew better than him about how he needed to run his life.

Sam stood the pitchfork against thc barn wall and walked up to Skip's stall. The horse stopped eating and nickered softly. Sam lightly scratched him between the ears. "Good ole Skip, guess you kinda had a workout today boy. You deserve somethin special for doin' such a good job. In the mornin', when the boy comes down, I'll fix you up with a treat."

He closed the barn doors and walked back to the house, still thinking about the day. It started out a little rough, then good, then ended rough. Maybe tomorrow's breakfast would start over better, though likely there'd be some prayin' goin' on. For now, he would eat left over pie and coffee for dinner, then head to bed. He wondered what Napoleon would do in this situation.

"What did you say to Sam, Alvin? He looked like a bee stung his rear end."

Alvin finished off the blackberry pie, at least what was left after the boys and Gennie got through.

"Oh, he got his feelins' up in a dander talkin' about that housekeeper of his. I think he doesn't want to admit it, that he likes her. He sure did put up a fuss about her wantin' to say grace over breakfast."

"She told me about that. Sounds to me like he's having to get used to having a strong female around, all over again, especially a pretty one. I don't believe he knows how to act around an unattached, pretty widow woman. It would be like watching a whirlwind, waiting to figure out if you're going to be sucked in or thrown out. He's just a little mixed up right now."

"All's, I said was, he might be set in his ways and a woman could make things easier for him. I didn't know he was gonna get all sideways about it. I think Mrs. Martin might be stirrin' up a hornet's nest inside ole Sam. She gets too close, and he'll likely leave her with a stinger."

"Well, I think you ought to apologize to him, I sure would hate to have him be upset with us. I'm just getting to know Hannah, and I'd like to keep her as a friend. If that means keeping Sam happy then we'll just have to work it out. By the way, I wanted to talk to you about Gennie going back to school. Hannah's boy Jacob was going to school regular in Nightshade and she asked if Jacob and Gennie could hitch a ride together. You wouldn't have to miss one of the boys from the farm, since Gennie wouldn't be alone with Jacob riding with her. They could use one of the mules when you could spare it, or maybe Sam wouldn't mind lending one of his mules too."

"Might be. Let me study on it a day or two then I'll tell ya what I think. It might work out to benefit everybody."

# CHAPTER 34

Jacob woke up to the sound of pots and pans banging from the kitchen. He rubbed his eyes, scratched his head and slowly drug himself up off the bed. Today he would be helping Mr. Anderson with the horses. He was eager to help saddle and bridle them. He might even ask Mr. Anderson if he could sit in the saddle and be lead around for a bit. For now, he had to get dressed and go collect eggs.

Jacob handed the eggs to Hannah. She took them from him and gave him a little squeeze. It was good to see him happy. He took it so hard when Jack died. They both cried for weeks. After the crying was over, she sent him back to his own bed but checked on him throughout the night for the first few days. He looked so sweet when he slept. Jacob had done a lot of growing since then. Not just in stature, but in confidence. Seeing how he looked around Mr. Anderson was well worth her putting up with any nonsense from the man. She could tell Mr. Anderson liked Jacob around too. Sam had been kind, thoughtful, and caring at first. And if they hadn't had a little disagreement at breakfast yesterday, she would have gone on thinking so. Still, she hadn't figured on him being so impertinent about saying grace. Even Jack in his drunkenness, never fussed about it. And he, though not often, prayed once or twice when they were together. When he was home from sea, they went to church together. Of course, as the drinking wore on, it was less and less. And yet she had to say, with Mr. Anderson, there might be something there to work with. Just a small crack in the dam. Sometimes a crack is the first sign of bigger things to come. Maybe she'd help it along. If she could stay at the job that is. It wasn't going to be easy for either one of them.

Hannah brought the milk jug with her to Sam's house for breakfast. This time when she knocked on the door, Sam invited her in and offered a cup of coffee. Maybe he was calling a truce. She accepted it and drank from the cup as she made her way to the kitchen. Jacob went into the library, book in hand to find a spot to curl up and read.

"Thank you for the coffee Mr. Anderson, I didn't see any at the house or I would have made a pot before I came here."

"Not likely to find coffee there, the Daltons didn't drink much of it. Serita only drank it when I made a pot, so I guess it's just a habit for me to have a few extra cups available. If you'd like to keep some, put it on the supply list and I"ll get it for you next trip to Nightshade. By the way, it might be easier for you and the boy to eat breakfast here instead of cookin' it twice every mornin'. That is if you have a mind to."

"Oh no, it's fine. I don't drink that much either, but it's nice to share a cup with you. But if you don't mind sharing your breakfast with us, that would help. I know Jacob would like to, and it would make things easier."

"Um Mrs. Martin. About yesterday. I didn't mean to be so bold with you, but I'm not keen to bein' put in a spot that requires me to change my normal ways. Serita was with me for over fifteen years and we butted heads sometimes but it weren't on the first day. So, I guess I'm sayin' sorry bout that. I'll try to be less stubborn if you try to be less bossy."

Hannah was wondering if there was an apology somewhere in his words. It sounded like he was apologizing but it could have been an insult too. Not sure how she should respond so she just replied,

"Well, I didn't mean to be bossy Mr. Anderson, just as I'm sure you didn't mean to be stubborn; Let's just try and work together for the sake of getting through our day without any battle scars, shall we?"

Sam nodded his head. "Well for the sake of peace, I'll try and keep mine. Just don't expect me to be actively participatin' in prayers over my food, but you and the boy are welcome to. By the way, if you'd like I can take you out for a look over of the Triple S when you're ready to."

"Sounds fair to me. Mr. Anderson. A ride out on the range, would be a nice gesture on your behalf. We'll work out a day to do just that. For now, I'll just finish up my coffee here and get started on your breakfast."

She noticed the blackberry pie was already gone. Guess that was last night's dinner.

She laughed a little wondering about how well that pie went down considering it had been prayed over.

She didn't notice her laugh caught Sam's attention. He couldn't figure out if she was laughing at him or not. He caught himself under his breath, stopping from saying what he was thinking. Nope he had other things to deal with today. May as well save that for another time.

Hannah thought to herself, looks like the Lord won the battle so far. Could be a few more left to be fought.

"Goin' out to the barn Mrs. Martin. See ya in a while for breakfast."

# CHAPTER 35

Sam stepped into the library to see Jacob absorbed in reading Gulliver's Travels. He tapped him gently on the shoulder to get his attention.

"I'm headed out to the barn Jacob, you comin'. I got a carrot treat here for Skip you can give it to him if you'd like to."

Jacob set the book down. "I'm ready Mr. Anderson. Can I help saddle and bridle today?"

"I'll get ya started but it's gonna take practice. Just have to be patient son, there's plenty of time for learnin'. I'm still learnin' myself. Come on, let's get goin."

Sam put Skip and Sable out to pasture, the evening before. There were three new horses, waiting in the stalls when Sam and Jacob walked in the barn.

"Where are Skip and Sable?"

"It's Skip and Sable's turn out in the pasture. They'll graze for another few days, then I'll turn these horses back out to graze too. You got one picked out for us today, Jacob?"

"Which one would you choose Mr. Anderson?"

"Well, they're all three good horses, but I think for today we oughta go with Banner. He's the oldest horse on the ranch and he's good about knowin' how to act around a greenhorn."

"What's a greenhorn?"

"That's somebody that don't know much about much. I spect that would be you boy."

"I won't be a greenhorn long, right?"

"Ok here ya go boy" Sam handed Jacob the lead rope motioning for him to step forward to Banner's stall.

Jacob held up the rope, just as he had the day before and walked Banner out to Sam at the hitching post.

Sam handed him a brush. "You brush him down as much as you can there boy. This one's a little taller than Sable". He picked up a metal bucket, turning it on its end and stood Jacob on top.

"Now, you oughta be able to reach up there a ways. When you're done, here's the blanket, goes on next."

While Jacob was brushing down Banner, Sam filled the other horses feed bins with cracked corn. "How ya doin' there son?"

Jacob loved the smell of the barn, the sweetness of fresh hay, the leather from the tack, and the cedar woodwork of the stall floors. Mama was right, it was gonna be good living here with Mr. Anderson. It was even better now that he could be around all the ranch animals. Not to mention, he had found a new friend in Gennie Lowoods. Maybe Mr. Anderson would teach him to ride, so when school started, he could drive him and Gennie to school.

"I'm finished Mr. Anderson, ya wanna come look?"

Sam ran his hands down the back of the horse and legs. "Looks good to me boy. Now can you throw the blanket over him?"

"Yes sir." Sam handed him a brown saddle blanket. Jacob stepped up on the bucket that Sam placed for him and threw the blanket over the back of Banner positioning it just right.

"This way Mr. Anderson?"

"That's it son. Now you watch me saddle up. You'll be doin' this pretty soon yourself."

Sam picked up the saddle from the ground, throwing it over his strong shoulders and heaving it over the back of the horse. He pulled the girth off the saddle horn, slipping it under the horse's belly and gave it a tug, tightening it until the horse made a slight groan.

"You see, you have to get the girth tight because a horse can hold its breath to prevent a snug fit. If it's not snug, you'll find yourself on the ground before too long. Now watch how I bridle him."

Sam pulled the bridle down from the saddle horn, slipping the head latch over Banners head. "A horse will open its mouth once it feels the cold metal bit against its teeth. You don't have to force it, just a little pressure to make sure he knows it's there. Slip it in, buckle up the neck strap and you are ready to ride."

Jacob watched and listened intently, taking in every move Sam made. He dreamed of riding down the fence rows side by side him on Sable and Sam on Banner, looking for fence breaks and stray cattle. He hoped it wouldn't take that long to learn it all.

"Let's go, we got a lot of land to cover before we get back for your mama's breakfast."

Sam climbed up in the stirrups, settling in, then reaching for Jacob's hand he boosted him from the bucket, Jacob's foot pushing himself up in the stirrup and lifted him around behind him as they set off to ride fences.

# CHAPTER 36

Breakfast went without much incident. True to Sam's word, he made well during prayer and finished eating, leaving Hannah to wash up the dishes. She had the day planned where she'd stay busy with chores right up until supper, then back to completing the supply lists, taking in the laundry and finally dinner before leaving to go back home with Jacob. She didn't realize how much work would be involved with such a big house. But she actually liked keeping herself busy about the place. The grass green pastures and blue skies were like a painting, too unreal to be so beautiful. The house had lovely rooms filled with ornate furniture and furnishings. She wondered if Alvin Lowoods had carved any of the chairs she saw in the parlor. Star had shown her the rocking chair on their visit. He had a talent for woodworking, you'd never have thought it by looking at him. He was a wiry little thing, not tall and broad like Sam. He actually looked much older than Sam to her. At least he didn't have Sam's temperament. It was funny how they could be such friends, as opposites in nature as they both were to each other. She didn't know if that said something about Sam as much as it did Mr. Lowoods. Star was easy to talk to. It was almost like talking to Naomi. She planned on riding to church with the Lowoods coming up this Sunday that was only three days away. She would have to talk to Mr. Anderson about using the surrey to travel to Nightshade for the day. He did say that she was welcome to it. She hoped he hadn't changed his mind since he still seemed to have a sore spot. Hannah wasn't going to let whatever was bothering him affect her. She had to think about Jacob, they were there to do a job, live in peace, and make a home. There was going to be trouble up ahead somewhere though. She could just feel it. She planned on bringing the subject after dinner tonight. Confrontation usually sits better on a man when he has a full stomach.

She had just finished tidying up in the parlor when she heard Sam and Jacob come in. They were both talking about cows and horses, never noticing she was listening as they passed by her in the parlor. It felt good to know Jacob was getting on so well with Mr. Anderson. He needed a man to look up to. Naomi's husband Robert had helped a little, but he was busy with Naomi and the girls. Jack was at sea during most of Jacob's childhood and when he was at home, whiskey was at the top of his priorities. Now for the first time in a long time, Mr. Anderson was stepping in to fill a void that had been missing in Jacob's life. Could be it was going to fill a void in hers too. She stopped herself. Now why would she be thinking that? Better be getting on with fixing supper. The less to think about that man the better.

Sam and Jacob went into the library to talk more about cows and horses. He handed Jacob a book with drawings of horses.

"This book can answer a lot of your questions Jacob. Most of what you learn will be by experience, but it never hurts to learn from a book either."

"I haven't finished Gulliver's Travels yet Mr. Anderson. But can I look at this one sometimes too?"

"Sure. But this one needs to stay here in the library. When you finish with Gulliver, then you can take on another. There are books on raisin' cattle, buildin' fences, shoein' horses, how to grow grass hay, all kinds of things that are important to a rancher. For now, this book will help you get an idea about the basics of ranch livin', so that you'll know it if you wanna have a ranch of your own someday

The more you learn about livestock, the better you will be at it when that day comes."

"A ranch of my own? I want to know everything, Mr. Anderson. That is if you don't mind teaching me sir. I hope I can drive the herd in with you when you think I'm ready. A ranch of my own. I'll be just like you, riding the fences on my own horse."

Sam chuckled, "you're a long way from that right now boy, but you work hard every day, take care of your mama, keep readin' those books and you just might have a spread as big or bigger than the Triple S. Now let's go see if supper is ready."

Hannah had supper waiting for Sam and Jacob in the dining room. She sat down with them to eat, quietly holding her peace until there was a break in the conversation.

"Mr. Anderson, as you know I'll be off on Sunday, and I was wondering if you meant what you said about using the surrey to go to church. I told Star, Mrs. Lowoods, I'd follow along with her if I decided to go. I'll make sure it gets back to you before evening and 'I'll return it to you well cleaned."

"Mrs. Martin I'm a man of my word and you are free to drive the surrey Sunday. I do have a suggestion though. I mentioned the other day about takin' a ride out over the Triple S. You may want to familiar yourself with the horses, I know Saturday is your half day, would you and Jacob be interested in takin' a horse ride with me to show you around the ranch? You might enjoy getting' away out in the open skies for a bit."

"Yes, seems we were just talking about that. The last time I was on a horse was in West Virginia. I miss it. I just need a change of clothes, after I finish up breakfast Saturday. Yes, I'd be interested Mr. Anderson. Thank you for asking."

"You ought to ride Sable mama, she is my favorite. Can she ride Sable Mr. Anderson?"

"I think you got some horse sense there Jacob, Sable and your mama might do good together. "You can ride with me or your mama, either way we'll count it a day."

"Count it a day Jacob."

"Count it a day mama."

# CHAPTER 37

Hannah was a little nervous about the deal she made with Sam. Not so much about riding, even though it had been a while since she straddled a horse, but more so seeing Sam in a role other than her employer. She wasn't sure what to expect from him or what he expected of her. At least Jacob would be there if things got too uncomfortable. She was surprised that he would even think of asking her, he hadn't really noticed her other than the few times he spoke to her since visiting the Lowoods.

She had to admit she did want to see the ranch up close. The ride would give her a chance to do that. Jacob was never one to give up a day spending time outdoors around horses or cows. She wouldn't have to talk much, she sure wasn't expecting much out of Sam in the way of pleasant conversation. Well, it might be a good opportunity to get to know him a little better. It definitely would be a nice day to spend the outdoors with Jacob.

Jacob woke up before Hannah did. He was excited about the day and barely slept the night before. He was all dressed and had the eggs collected waiting on her to kiss him good morning.

Hannah decided to wear her old pair of trousers for the ride. No sense in taking a change of clothes. She would just wear her apron for cooking breakfast then freshen up after the ride. She chose a blue cotton blouse, pulled her hair back with a black ribbon and topped with a blue bonnet. Her riding pants were a little snug, but still loose enough to be comfortable in the saddle. Another nice day outside, she hoped it would stay that way.

"Well look at you son. You're all up and ready for the day. Did you sleep well?'

'I slept a little, but I'm plenty awake now. I never seen you wear long leg pants mama. You look real pretty in them."

"I only wear them when I plan on sitting on a horse for half the day. But thank you for saying so. Did you put the eggs up?"

"Yes, I put them in the egg basket. Are we ready to go now?"

"Oh, I suppose. I'll just wear a bonnet to ride. I don't have a cowboy hat like Mr. Anderson. Maybe next time in town I'll do a little shopping and get us both a hat. Might come in handy for another ride someday."

"I want one that looks like Mr. Anderson's please."

"We'll see son. Come on, I have to fix breakfast for a couple of hungry cowboys."

Hannah and Jacob were met at the door by Sam and his cup of coffee. He stared at Hannah seeing her hair pulled back in a bonnet, just the way it was on their first trip from Nightshade. How was he going to make it through the ride without keeping his eyes off her? Well, he would just have to keep a conversation going somehow so the eye contact wouldn't be misconstrued as gawking. This was just a leisure ride to get to know the horse, and show her the Triple S. The only way to understand the beauty of it was on horseback on a fair spring day. Jacob understood it, why shouldn't his mama have an opportunity to see what a ranch is all about. It didn't hurt that he was to be accompanied by a handsome young woman.

"Good mornin', come in Mrs. Martin, Jacob. I see you're dressed for our ride today, Mrs. Martin. It's gonna be a good day for it."

"I was hoping it would be. I know Jacob was too. He barely slept a wink last night; he was so excited for today."

"Plenty of time for that. I have coffee on the stove if you like. I'll just go get the horses ready while you're in the kitchen. Then we'll head out to see the land. Jacob you wanna help with the horses?"

"Yes sir. I'm ready."

"Alright get on a goin', I'm right behind ya."

Sam grabbed his hat from the hat rack and turned back to

Hannah. She was already busy in the kitchen putting on her apron. He watched as she pulled the apron tight around her waist. He caught himself smiling, and quickly turned his attention back to Jacob. He hoped Hannah hadn't seen him. But Jacob did and he gave a puzzled look to Sam.

"Just makin' sure your mama found her apron, boy. Let's go now."

# CHAPTER 38

There was little talk between Sam and Hannah at the breakfast table. Jacob, however, had no problem keeping a conversation going with himself. He kept Hannah and Sam updated with his summary of Gulliver's Travels and the adventures of Lilliput. Then he told them all about his plans for school, what books he wanted to read, how he was going to own a ranch someday. With the kitchen cleaned and dishes put away, Hannah met Sam and Jacob in the library where both of them were deep in conversation about why Angus cows were healthier than longhorns.

"I'm all done in the kitchen. Are we ready for a horse ride?"

"Yes mam, Jacob, show your mama the way to the barn."

"Come on mama, you'll love Sable."

"What a pretty name for a horse, I can't wait to see her."

Together hand in hand Jacob led Hannah while Sam followed behind. As they made their way to the barn door, Sable stuck her head over the stall door and nickered softly when Jacob walked into the barn. She was a pretty little thing, Hannah thought. She would expect no less from any of the livestock Mr. Anderson was responsible for.

Sam pulled the saddles from the tack room while Jacob led Sable out of the stall. He tied her to the hitching post and pulled a bucket up to brush her.

"I see you've done this before Jacob. Looks like Mr. Anderson has a new helper now."

"I'm big enough now mama, pretty soon I'll be putting the saddle on too."

Sam looked at him sternly, "Now hold up their partner, you ain't that big yet. These saddles can be heavy for a grown man like me, you keep on doin' what you're doin' and it won't be long before you'll be swingin' yourself right up there on your own horse one day soon."

"That's right son, now you watch your mama show you how she does it. May I Mr. Anderson?"

Sam raised his eyebrows and tilted his head in surprise. "Well mam, if you think you don't need any help I'll just stand back and watch."

Hannah picked up the saddle and blanket, then threw it over the back of the horse. She pulled the girt and cinched it snug. Then she lengthened the stirrups, to her long legs and put the bridle over Sable's head, settling the bit in between the teeth.

"Well, I see you haven't forgotten how to tack up a horse. Pretty impressive if I may say so."

"You may." She put her foot in the stirrup and swung over landing solidly in the seat." Now Jacob, come here and I'll pull you up behind me."

"Oh no mam, I'll be happy to give him a boost. Come on boy." Sam lifted Jacob up and over Sable in one motion.

"I think we will just walk her around the barn, while you get saddled Mr. Anderson."

"Alright, I'll be right with ya then."

Sam finished tacking up Skip and met Hannah and Jacob outside the barn.

"Just follow me Mrs. Martin, might be a good long ride today. There's a waterin' hole about half mile out, we'll stop there and give the horses a break on the way back. I'll take you to the top of the ridge. That's the best place to see the real Triple S. All I ask is you keep up and don't get behind, I'd hate to have to go lookin' for ya."

"You go right ahead Mr. Anderson, Jacob and I will stay right beside you. Sable, you say.

Get up Sable." She gave the mare a slight nudge with her knee and with a giddy up, Sable lazily walked out of the barn into the sunshine of the barnyard.

Hannah had forgotten how peaceful it could be on horseback. As a little girl, she rode almost every day. It was a time she could forget about cares of the day even at a young age. She hoped Jacob would be able to experience riding one day. This would be the perfect place to learn. Evidently Mr. Anderson was already starting him out. She watched him as he rode his horse in front of her. He sure did sit in the saddle well. She thought he actually seemed to be enjoying the day with them. He didn't seem irritated and grumpy like he was after the visit to the Lowoods yesterday. She thought to herself she kind of liked this, Sam Anderson.

The Triple S looked even more beautiful on horseback. The rolling hills against the bright blue skies and pearly white clouds were breath taking. The cows barely paid attention as they rode past. Hannah saw the rest of the ranch horses mixing in with the cows grazing on grass. The heifers and calves huddled together under the grove trees. One of the horses lifted his head and whinnied, stomping his feet as if he were calling them to come to attention. Sam stopped to point it out.

"That's Comanche. He's the stallion on the Triple S. He's makin' sure Sable and Skip know he's in charge. Pay him no never mind, that's the job of a stallion. He's always lookin' to stir up trouble, so's he can let the other horses know whose boss."

Hannah raised up in the saddle slightly to get a better look, "He's beautiful, spirited, but beautiful."

"Oh, he would agree with you about that. Sable had a colt out of him a few years back. It looked just like him. I sold him to a Quaker in Mountain Pine. I heard he's pullin' a buggy for their family. I bet I'd hardly recognize him now if I saw him."

"Mr. Anderson, will Sable have another colt sometime?"

"I been thinkin' about it. She's a good mare. Maybe I'll put her out with Comanche this summer, she should have a colt by the end of summer next year, if everything works out."

"Come on, I'll take you over to the south pasture, that's where the steers are. I keep them separated from the cows, because the old bull likes to fight with 'em. Plus, it's easier to have 'em all together when we round em up for auction twice a year."

Sam gave Skip a little kick, speeding up to a fast walk.

Hannah turned to Jacob. "Hang on Jacob, we're gonna speed up a little to keep with Mr. Anderson."

"Oh, Mr. Anderson does that when I ride with him too. I'm hanging on mama."

"Oh, so you've been riding huh?"

"Well… Ummm, I, ummm So umm... Mr. Anderson said he was my age when he rode his first horse. Sides, Uncle Robert let me brush his horse and one time he let me sit on it."

Hannah and Sam were now side by side. The horses were nipping playfully at each other as their strides matched beat to beat.

"Now mam, the boy ain't the problem here. "I could see he had his heart set on ridin' and to tell you the truth by his age I could handle a horse with no problems. I was right there with him the whole time and I promise you I wouldn't gonna let nothin' happen to him. You can just blame me and not the boy."

"Mr. Anderson, I'd appreciate it that in the future that you discuss with me first your intentions regarding anything about Jacob. What you did as a child isn't my concern, but my son is. I just want assurances that from now on you talk to me first about these things when you heard me tell him not to ride."

"Well mam, if memory serves, you told him not to bug me about ridin', you didn't say he couldn't ride. With all due respect of course."

Hannah had to admit, she had him on that one.

"So that we understand each other then, Jacob from now on you mind what I say, and Mr. Anderson, you aren't to ignore me when I expect my son to mind me. Is that clear?"

Both Sam and Jacob at the same time." Yes mam."

"Sorry mam. He's a good little feller. Hope this doesn't cause any hard feelins' between us."

"Let's just enjoy the rest of the day for now if you don't mind?"

Hannah gave a little kick to Sable, at first the mare threw her head back and seemed to balk but then when Hannah clicked, she picked her pace causing her to be slightly ahead of and in front of Sam. Sam did the same, catching up with them before both horses settled back into a lazy walk. Sam pulled Skip to a stop on top on a high ridge overlooking the south pasture and motioned for Hannah to do the same.

Looking down from a ridge overlooking the ranch, started to put things into perspective for Hannah.

She pulled her bonnet back letting it dangle from the back of her neck. She could see why Sam loved the Triple S. so much. Hundreds of cows were grazing, lingering at times in one spot, then moving slowly to the next patch of green grass, only lifting their heads up occasionally to gaze into the distance, while lazily chewing each clump. There were rolling green hills and pasture for as far as the eye could see. It was peaceful, so much so that she closed her eyes for a few seconds and took in a deep breath.

"It's beautiful Mr. Anderson. Hard to believe this is real and not a picture painting."

Sam took his hat off, hanging it on the saddle horn to rest. He leaned far back in the saddle just as Skip relaxed his hips, shifting its back end to one side as a soldier at ease, loosening the load he was bearing.

"Yep, even after all of these years of livin' on the Triple S, I'd say I get the same feelin'. Ain't nothin' as pretty as green pasture and blue skies. All those are pure bred Angus, each one sired by a generation before. They all come from bulls and heifers born, raised and died here clear back to my great grandfather's first herd. I never get tired of lookin at 'em." Makes you kinda humble, knowing there's things that stay the same in this old world. Even after time passes by. It's a good feelin' to know there are some things you can still count on and that means a whole lot to a man like me."

Jacob twisted himself around to get a better look at the cattle in the pasture.

"If I ate grass all day, would I be as fat as one of those cows Mr. Anderson?"

"Well, I tell ya Jacob, a cow has four stomachs, they eat all day every day and fill up with grass which is like you eatin' a sugar cube, only you have one stomach. If you ate sugar all day every day and didn't go out, jump around or play, you'd be fat too. A cow doesn't do much but eat and sleep so all the sugar, stored in their stomachs just turns into fat."

Jacob was a little puzzled, "So I have one stomach to fill, and a cow has four? That's how come they eat so much?"

Hannah giggled thinking about what it would be like if Jacob had four stomachs.

They lingered for a while enjoying the sunshine and discussing the benefits of ranch life along with the events that brought them together in the moment.

"Well, I guess we better be turnin' back Mrs. Martin, you can get on with the rest of the day, and I'm sure you want to rest up for Sunday. I'll have the surrey ready for you to take in the mornin', you just come get it when you're ready for it."

"Thank you, Mr. Anderson, I really appreciate you showing me the ranch. And thanks for using the surrey. I'll have it back tomorrow afternoon. I may visit with Star a little after church if that's okay, I'll bring it back right after."

"That's fine. We'll just walk the horses back to the barn and give them a cool down. Jacob when we get back can you brush 'em down and put 'em in their stalls."

"Yes sir."

They turned the horses back down the hill, walking them side by side. Stopping only once at the creek to give the horses a drink. The conversation back to the barn was small talk about the upcoming auction and the plans for getting supplies.

After untacking the horses and feeding them in their stalls, Sam and Hannah along with Jacob walked back to the main house.

"I'll have the surrey ready for you Mrs. Martin, if that will do for ya."

"Yes, thank you Mr. Anderson, guess Jacob and I will be on our way home now. Jacob and I enjoyed the ride today. Thank you for the company."

# CHAPTER 39

Hannah walked home from the main house, holding Jacob's hand and listening to him talk on and on about cows' stomachs. She was half listening to him and half thinking about the ride this morning. Sam Anderson was a complicated man. But she was struck how easy he was to be around as they rode along the pasture on horseback. Jacob definitely saw him as a hero and looked up to him as a man. Not a bad thing, but it could get tricky over time. True, Mr. Anderson was a self-made man, seemed likeable to the neighbors and definitely passionate about the Triple S. Still, something didn't set right with her about his aversion to praying or going inside the helpers' quarters. She learned from Star that Mr. Anderson's parents were involved with the church when he was a child. But when his father left as war broke out, he took on the ranch responsibilities and limited his church going. The whole Amelia thing pretty much hit him hard and even though both his parents continued to attend, Sam never returned to church.

She replayed the conversation she had with Star about Sam's attitude after the break-up with his fiancé.

"Sam pretty much just dried up as a man. He was cordial to people, but you knew that he always seemed to be sitting on a burr to his backside. It didn't take much for him to just fester and sully up when he was annoyed about something. I can't tell you how many times Alvin and him rubbed each other wrong about something silly and Sam would just stomp off in a huff. Of course, it always blows over in a day or two and it's back to the same. Alvin just ignores it; they know each other too well to keep a dust up between them."

Hannah knew what Star was talking about. She saw it a few times already, just being around him for a few days.

Well, might as well just take it in stride and not try to cause aggravation as much as possible. But one thing, Sam would sure benefit from knowing about the Lord. Maybe she could work on that and keep her job too.

Jacob and Hannah spent the rest of the day planting a small vegetable garden in the front yard. She kept a few seeds from West Virginia just in case someday there was an opportunity to use them.

She found a hoe in one of the sheds in back of the house. Ms. Serita must have had her own garden here before. The ground was rich and perfect for growing things. She hoed the trenches while Jacob planted the seeds. Corn, turnips, tomatoes, potatoes. After covering the seeds up, she found a little fence wire to put around everything to help keep out the cows or other critters.

"Let's go get some rest Jacob. It's been a long day; we have to get up early for church tomorrow."

"Are we going with Mr. and Mrs. Lowoods in the morning mama?"

"We won't be riding with them, but we will be riding in Mr. Anderson's surrey along beside them."

"Will I get to see Gennie then?"

"I expect so son, she's a pretty thing, isn't she?"

"Aww, I guess for a girl she could be. I just like the way she talks, its sounds a little like the way Mrs. Lowoods talks."

"That's because Mrs. Lowoods is part English Jacob. Her mother was from the country of Great Britain far away."

"Well, I'll just be glad when I can go to school again. I'm gonna let Gennie read the book Mr. Anderson gave me when I finish it. Gennie said she hasn't read about Gulliver."

"Just make sure it's all right with Mr. Anderson son. I'm sure Gennie will enjoy it just like you do. Set out your church going clothes for the morning. It will be here for you know it". She kissed him on the cheek, patted his behind and watch him skip his way off to his room. That boy was a blessing to her, through all the obstacles she had been through, Jacob was the one thing that kept her hopeful for the future.

Hannah changed into her night gown, got into bed and read her Bible from the book of Colossians:

Make allowance for each other's faults and forgive the person who offends you. Use God's words to teach and counsel each other.

Well that seemed appropriate considering what she was up against. But Hannah knew it wasn't just Sam Anderson the words were talking about. She herself was having trouble forgiving Jack. She thought she had forgiven him, but if she were true to herself and the word of God, she still had some blame for the life she was put in now.

Maybe, God was trying to teach and counsel her in this moment of life. Maybe he was using Sam Anderson to teach her something about that, but maybe she was being used to teach him about life too.

She closed her Bible, setting it gently on the bedside table and blew out the light. As she lay in the darkness, she prayed for wisdom to deal with Sam and to raise Jacob in the right way. But most of all to teach her the way to forgiveness in all things according to the word.

# CHAPTER 40

Sam finished up his outside chores by cleaning out barn stalls and tack. He made his way back to the main house thinking about his ride with Hannah. Kind of surprised him how well she handled Sable. Could be a lot of things that might surprise him the more he got to know her. Something about that woman bugged him. Not sure what it was, but it bugged him. What made matters worse was she was smart and had pretty eyes. That spelled trouble. He was gonna have to make it a point keep his distance from her, but it was going to be hard not to stay close to the boy. He kind of liked having that little rascal around. Had to be just business with the woman though.

He finished up the leftovers that Hannah had made that day. And took with him a cup of coffee as he pulled out a copy of Robinson Crusoe. He had read the book as a child but thought it might be too complicated for Jacob to read just now. Maybe next year, that is, as long as Hannah was still around, he'd offer it up to him.

Funny, about that Crusoe. He could relate. A castaway living on a remote island, relying on his own wits to survive. Sort of like his life the past few years. He did have Serita and the Lowoods as friends, so not much to compare there. But it was as if the Triple S was the island, and he was using his wits to help survive.

Sam made it through the first two chapters, but his eyelids were getting heavy. He finished off half a cigar, put the book back in the bookcase and made his way upstairs to bed.

Tomorrow he would get up early to have the surrey ready for

Hannah. Then he would plan to spend the rest of Sunday, shoeing horses and checking for new calves. By then Ms. Hannah should be ready to come home. And that was what he was thinking about as he drifted off to sleep.

# CHAPTER 41

"Jacob, wake up. We have to get ready for church."

Jacob rolled over on his side but didn't seem to be making any effort to actually get out of bed.

"Jacob, don't you want to see Gennie this morning?"

. He slowly rolled out of bed and onto the wood floor, stretching and yawning.

"I'm up mama. Are we going to meet the Lowoods on the way to church?"

"Yes, after we pick up the surrey from Mr. Anderson. Go wash your face and put on clean clothes. I'll have breakfast ready for you when you're done."

Hannah thought about meeting Sam again while eating breakfast. She was lost in thought and didn't hear Jacob when he asked about which horse was Mr. Anderson going to use for the surrey.

"Mama, which horse?"

"What. What did you say son?"

"Which horse will Mr. Anderson use for the surrey. I hope it's Skip, I like the way he tosses his head when he trots."

"Oh well I expect Mr. Anderson will know which one is best for the surrey. Are you done eating? We should be heading over to pick it up."

Sam was already with the surrey when Hannah and Jacob found him in front of the main house. He had Skip, just like Jacob thought, all hitched up and ready.

"Good mornin', folks, looks like it gonna be a nice day for the both of you to be on a buggy ride this clear Sunday mornin'. Mrs. Martin, Skip here will mind your reinin' but just in case, he does have a little perk to his ways, so if you see him goin' a little faster than your wantin', just pull a little tighter on the rein and he'll get back to walkin' pace. I only ask that you have him back here before late afternoon so I can pasture him to rest before sundown. Otherwise, he's good to go to and from Nightshade and home."

"Okay, sounds good Mr. Anderson, I like a horse with a little spirit. We should be able to handle him just fine. We'll be back directly after church. Should be after supper time. Thank you so much for letting us borrow him and the surrey. I told Star that I would meet her at their farm and trail behind. I already know some folks at church, we went there with my cousin Naomi, so I'm looking forward to seeing everyone again. You know you're welcome to ride along if you wanted."

Sam shifted uneasily from one foot to the other.

"Well now mam that is nice of you to ask but I planned on doin' some chores on the farm today, so I don't think I'll be goin' with ya. You go on though, I hope you have a nice day at the Lowoods, and church. Let me help you up in the buggy."

Sam offered his hand to Hannah and helped lift her up to the bench seat. She noticed his hands were a little rough and calloused. Hands of a working man. He lifted her as if she were light as a feather. He was so strong. Then he reached for Jacob and lifted him up to sit beside her on the seat.

"All right Mr. Anderson thank you again. We'll see you later." She clicked to Skip and gave a gentle slap of the reins, and true to Skip's name, he tossed his head before striking out to a brisk walk.

Jacob turned in his seat to see Sam waving goodbye. Hannah could see him out of the corner of her eye. She thought his face seemed a little sad as they drove away.

Jacob waved back. "Bye Mr. Anderson, see you later."

# CHAPTER 42

Star and Alvin, along with the boys and Gennie, were all getting into their wagon, when Hannah pulled up.

"Good morning, Hannah, Jacob." Star sitting by Alvin's side was dressed in a cream-colored cotton dress with a matching hat. "Say good morning to the Martins, boys."

"Good morning Mrs. Martin. Jacob," the boys in unison and Alvin just a tip of the hat.

"Good morning, Jacob." Gennie was perched in between Alvin and Star, and she had to peek around them both to see Jacob.

"Say good morning to the Lowoods Jacob."

Jacob was a little embarrassed. He was singled out by Gennie, but he offered back a half-hearted good morning anyway.

"Jacob and I will just follow behind you all to church if that's okay."

Alvin tipping his hat again, "Sure thing Mrs. Martin, we should get there just in time for services."

"When we get back Hannah, I'd be happy if you and little Jacob there would eat supper with us. I have pork chops set out and finish it up with mash potatoes, gravy, biscuits and turnip greens."

"That sounds delicious, you must let me help with the cooking though. I can fix up the mashed potatoes while you handle the pork and turnip greens. Jacob can help by cutting up the potatoes."

"No need for it but if you want to help out, I won't say no. Gennie and Jacob can both cut up the potatoes. We better get moving on or we will be late for church.

Hannah and the Lowoods both arrived at Nightshade Community Church, greeting the other church members as they walked through the chapel doors. Horse and buggies were lined up and tied to trees and hitching posts. Everyone had their Sunday best clothes on, from the starchiest pair of overalls, leather Stetsons and shiny boots worn by the menfolk to the laciest dresses and high bonnets worn by the women. The little boys wearing string ties were tugging at their collars, little girls were swishing their lace skirts and prancing around each other giggling, only to be shushed by parents as each family took their seats on wooden pews.

Hannah saw Naomi and Robert sitting with their girls near the front.

"Star, would you mind if I sit up front with my cousin Naomi? I'm sure she wants to hear about how we are doing, and we have a few minutes before service starts."

"Land sakes no girl, go on. With these rowdy boys of mine the last place for them to be is up front where the pastor can glare at them. Jacob and Gennie can sit together if you don't mind. You go on, we'll meet up after church and Alvin and I will wait on you."

"I'll meet up with you then after church. Go on with Ms. Star, Jacob." As she finished talking, she looked up just in time to see Naomi waving for her to come sit by them.

Naomi stood up as Hannah made her way over and reached out to hug her as she took her place on the pew.

"Hannah, it's so good to see you. I've been wondering how you and Mr. tall rancher man were getting along." Naomi gave her a wink.

"We're doing fine Naomi. It's been a little bumpy to say the least, but we're working on trying to figure out each other's ways. Although Mr. Anderson is a little bit set in his."

"Well Robert and I had talked about traveling out to see you, but we weren't sure if it would be too soon."

"I told Naomi I thought it might be better to come in the fall," Robert said." I have a lull in my practice around that time. I could shut the office down without too much trouble and by then it might be easier for you and Mr. Anderson."

"Mr. Anderson runs cattle to the stockyards in late fall, but maybe come early fall. I would love to visit with you all then. Oh, here comes Reverend Mayweather. We can talk about it after services if that's okay?"

Naomi and Robert both nodded as the reverend made his way up to the pulpit. The members all bowed their heads as he led them in morning prayer and then Sunday sermon.

# CHAPTER 43

Reverend Mayweather greeted everyone at the door as they made their way out of the building.

Most shook his hand and told him how they enjoyed the sermon, or a favorite hymn that was sung. He tried to shake every member's hand, but missed a few that snuck around the line, those avoiding a slight wait due to a chatty parishioner.

After services people were gathered outside in little groups, enjoying the sunshine and making small talk before each getting into buggies or climbing into a saddle to make the ride back to their own homes. Hannah caught Naomi and Robert up to date on events at the Triple S. She called Star and Alvin over to introduce them.

"Star, Alvin, this is my cousin Naomi and her husband Robert. They have two little girls around here somewhere."

Star reached out her hand to Naomi first then Robert. Alvin followed with the same.

"Nice to meet you Ms. Naomi, Alvin and I have seen you and Mr. Robert in church occasionally. It's nice to finally be able to put a name to a stranger."

"Nice to meet you both too. We know a few people from church but hadn't got around to meeting everybody. We mostly just know the folks living in Nightshade, but you both don't live far from Mr. Anderson I'm guessing."

"No, we don't., I don't get up to Nightshade much since I'm busy trying to keep up with four stubborn boys and a sassy little girl. But

Alvin and the boys do go to town every now and then as well has helping Mr. Anderson with the cattle runs."

Alvin nodded," I hear you're a dentist Mr. Sanders. I have a back tooth that's been bothering me a bit. Maybe I need to pay you a visit."

"You just come in whenever you can Mr. Lowoods. I'd be happy to take look at it for you."

"Well Naomi, I think I'd better be getting back. Mr. Anderson let me borrow the surrey today and I don't want to keep it out too long. I'll see you again soon. Love you."

As they made their goodbyes, Star and Alvin waved to the couple and headed off to collect the boys and Gennie. Hannah called out to Jacob who was sitting in a circle of boys with Gennie playing marbles.

"Let's go Jacob. We are stopping off at the Lowoods for lunch then back home."

Jacob jumped up and ran to give Naomi a hug before they left, catching up with Hannah as she climbed into the surrey.

"Okay Mama, let's go!"

# CHAPTER 44

After the blessing, Star passed around platefuls of pork chops, and mashed potatoes. Alvin and the boys had first choice then Hannah and Jacob. Gennie and Star were last to partake.

There was plenty of table talk during lunch and everybody had a good laugh when Alvin told them about the time when he was a boy out collecting eggs. He saw a very large snake in the chicken coop.

"I had my shotgun ready to shoot em when I felt something crawling up my leg inside my overalls. Now in my head I was sure that snake had gotten to me. So, I begun whoopin' and hollerin' jumpin' up and down. I ran faster than a brass bullet out of that chicken coop pullin' off my overalls at the same time. As soon as I got them off a big ole moth flew right out. And me standin' there naked as a jaybird. But I promise you, in the end that old snake got his."

"Oh Alvin, you've told that story a thousand times. But I got to admit, it's still a pretty funny thought of you shucking those overalls and the look you probably had on your face when you saw that moth."

Hannah helped Star put all the dishes away and straighten up the kitchen after the meal. They were seated alone at the table while Alvin and the boys went to feed the animals, Gennie and Jacob went to play on the swing.

"Well Hannah, looks like you've made it alive so far living around Sam Anderson. The last time he was here he left in a little cloud of smoke over his head. Alvin told me he thought it had to do with you somehow. I swear that man just seems like he's afraid to be human sometimes. But I do believe you may be just what he needs, to break that old shell of his. It took Serita years to get his trust. It's looking like it may be sooner for you."

"Star, I'm not sure about that, and I'm not sure if I even would want to try. From what I've seen so far, he's got a twenty- foot wall built around himself. Once or twice, I think I've caught him peeking over it. Likely will take some time to trust me. And it sure would make life easier for everybody if he would get over the wall. But for now, I'll just focus on earning my keep, raise Jacob, and plan for his future. When and if Mr. Anderson, decides to trust again, it will more likely be the Lord and not me that gets his attention. Speaking of which, I need to get Jacob ready and head back to the ranch. I told Mr. Anderson I'd have the surrey back after church, so I'm sure he's expecting us soon. Thank you so much for riding to church together and the wonderful meal. You really are a good neighbor, but I think you're a better friend."

"Aww shucks, Hannah. It's nice to have you as a neighbor and friend. I just feel like you and Sam are gonna be friends soon, maybe, you never know, could be even something more than that."

Hannah felt her cheeks flush a little with those words. She could only hope that they could be at least friends. At best? Well, she couldn't say what was best. Hannah hugged Star as they walked out to the front porch to call Jacob away from play and make the trip home. Home, that's what she had now, a home of her own. And as she had that thought, she silently gave thanks for the blessings in her life. Thankful for all that she had been blessed with, and for all the blessings to come.

# CHAPTER 45

Sam had been a little out of sorts all morning. Seems like it began right after, Ms. Martin and Jacob left for church. He couldn't quite put a finger on what was bothering him, but he knew something just wasn't sittin' right. Could be he was hungry. He had a light breakfast of coffee and cold biscuits. Ms. Martin was due back from church pretty soon he figured. She mentioned she might stop at the Lowoods for supper first. He pulled the pocket watch from its chain out of his vest to check the time. Yep, should be back anytime now.

He had finished cleaning stalls, riding the fences and checking on the herd. Well, he'd go in and take a hot bath, put on a clean shirt and get ready to meet Mrs. Martin and Jacob when they returned from the Lowoods. He was curious how church went. Well, no sense in wastin' time on it, may as well go get cleaned up.

Hannah and Jacob had been talking about church and the supper with the Lowoods on the way home to the Triple S.

"Were you happy to see Aunt Naomi and Uncle Robert today, Jacob?"

"Yes, maybe they will come visit us sometime mama. Lizzy and Jane could help feed the chickens too."

"We'll see Jacob. We might have to ask Mr. Anderson about that first just to make sure he won't mind. It's really his house you know."

"I thought it was our house?"

"Well, it is, and it isn't. See I work for Mr. Anderson, and he provides us with a place to live, that's part of the deal."

"Why doesn't he live there?"

"He lives in the main house. He has to be close to tend the cattle and horses. He built the house we are in a long time ago and just needs us to take care of it."

"Will he come and visit us sometime?"

"There really isn't a need for him to. I wonder if maybe he would come if I offered to fix a meal with us instead of eating at the main house. Would you like that?"

"Sure, but he kind of seemed sad when he got to the house."

"We might have to work on him a little bit. You just leave it to me. We are going to be neighborly neighbors if I have anything to say about it."

They pulled up to the main house just as Sam came out. It looked like he had just bathed, his hair was a little damp and he had shaved. As she stopped the surrey to climb down, he offered his hand to help. She could smell a light scent of soap and it reminded her of her father in the days working in the coal mines. He always was covered in coal soot, and it took him a long time of scrubbing with soap and water to get clean again.

"How was your trip Ms. Martin? Did Skip behave himself?"

"Oh, just fine. Reverend Mayweather gave a good sermon, and I had a chance to meet up with Naomi and Robert. We just finished having supper with Star and Alvin. She sent you some leftovers to eat if you're hungry. The pork chops are tasty."

Hannah reached back up into the surrey and pulled down the picnic basket Star had placed the leftovers in.

"I'll have to tell Star thank you next time I'm over. I gotta tell you my stomach has been growlin' a bit since breakfast this mornin'."

"Umm, Mr. Anderson? Jacob and I were just talking about maybe you coming to eat sometime with us at the quarters. It might be nice to eat in a different atmosphere than just having your meals at the same place, same time every day."

"I, I, ah, I, I'll think about it. Thank you for askin' me. We'll see."

"Is there a problem Mr. Anderson? Is it because I'm your employee, you're my employer?"

"Now Mrs. Martin. I have my own reasons that I'd like to keep to myself. It's not thata way. There are just some things that are hard to explain. Let's just keep things the way they are now if ya don't mind." Changing the subject, he asked if she would be needing anything more with the surrey before he put it up.

Hannah wondered about him, but she was determined not to give up. And once her mind was made up it would take more than a head strong rugged cowboy to do much more than tangle with a determined coal miners' daughter.

# CHAPTER 46

Hannah kept her schedule every morning treading up to the main house to clean, cook and keep the ledgers. Every so often Sam came to fetch her when it looked rainy, but she enjoyed the walks with just her and Jacob to tell the truth of it. Hannah, looked forward to seeing Sam. His face was less grim these days. She hadn't brought up the idea again of sharing a meal at the quarters house. Oh, he was still grumpy occasionally. And he tried her patience to its ends. She had to ask the Lord to help hold her tongue many times. That was somewhat of a challenge. Jacob had birthday coming up in a few weeks. Maybe a party. He and Gennie were out of school for the summer. It was a perfect time to have it. She could invite the Lowoods Naomi, Robert and the girls. But Sam?

# CHAPTER 47

"Mr. Anderson, I need to pick up a few things in town. Could I ride with you the next trip to Nightshade?"

Sam was entrenched, reading a book in the library. He closed the book slowly, took off his glasses setting the book across his lap and his glasses on the corner table. He looked up to see Hannah, tugging at her apron as she came in. She took a seat in the high back chair across from him.

"I'm headed out for supplies, day after tomorrow. Can it wait until then?"

"Yes, that's fine. I'd like to drop Jacob off at the Lowoods before we go. He has been asking to go and swim in the creek with Gennie and the Lowoods boys so, it would just be you and me if that's okay?"

Sam paused before answering. Just me and the woman? Couldn't be any harm in that.

Hannah noticed he seemed to be distracted and not responding to the question.

"Mr. Anderson?"

He was jarred out of his thinking by hearing his name.

"We'd have to leave right after sunrise."

"That won't be a problem. Jacob is so excited about swimming he probably won't even sleep the night before. I'll have him ready to go."

"We could eat breakfast in Nightshade no need for you to cook. 'Course Jacob might miss a meal. I think Star might would feed him though. All right, let's plan on it."

Hannah thought it might be a good time to bring up the birthday party on the trip to town.

While in Nightshade, she could pick up new clothes for Jacob. He was growing so much the pants were getting a little short. Maybe she would buy him a cowboy hat and boots for his birthday. Lots of things to be accomplished with this trip to Nightshade. In the meantime, she would plan on getting with the Lowoods and Naomi to invite them to the party. Star would surely agree to keep Jacob for the day. Her mind was racing. She had a lot to do.

The next morning Hannah woke Jacob up early, gathering his clothes for the day at the Lowoods.

"You and Mr. Anderson going to town mama? You going to shop too?"

"Yes, Jacob, I need to get a few things for the both of us in town. You don't mind spending the day with Ms. Star and Gennie, do you?"

"No, it will be fun to be around Matt, Mark, Luke and John." He winced, and maybe Gennie too, a little. "I'm glad Mr. Anderson is riding to town with you. He looks happier, I think. Don't you?"

"Well, his happy is a little different than what our happy is but yes, it's nice to see. And if you tell him I said that I'll swat your behind."

"You're teasing me right mama?"

"You just say something about it and see young man."

Hannah and Jacob made it to the main house right at daybreak. Sam already had the buckboard hitched up to the mules. He gave a smile as he greeted them good morning.

Sam turned to face Jacob "Well Jacob, are you ready to spend your day with the Lowoods? I hear you may get to swim a little today. Awful nice day to take a dip."

"Yea, Mark and Matt told me at church Sunday. We're gonna catch tadpoles. Are you and mama gonna be back before dark? I don't think they said for me to spend the night."

"Mr. Anderson and I will be back before dinner time. I want you to mind your manners while you're staying at the Lowoods. You hear me? Say yes mam and no mam when you're speaking to Mrs. Lowoods and offer to help set the supper table when its time."

"Yes mam. If you say so."

They dropped Jacob off at the Lowoods as Hannah thanked Star for letting him stay. Star seemed to know something because she winked at Hannah as Jacob ran off to catch up with the boys.

"Guess you two will be busy getting supplies and such, huh Hannah?"

"I have a few things I need to get for Jacob, Mr. Anderson was kind enough to let me tag along."

Sam, feeling uncomfortable discussing their plans, twisted a little in his seat. "Yep, we need to get a goin' now Star, we gotta get back before dinner. 'Appreciate you taken on little Jacob, he didn't have breakfast this mornin', but I figured you would take care of that."

"I'll fix him up. Sam, you and Hannah have a safe trip to town now. It's going to be a nice day for a buggy ride."

It seemed to be, Star had a bigger grin than usual, Sam thought to himself. He wasn't quite sure what to make of it.

"Go on now Star, don't you have something you need to be doin'? I expect to have Mrs. Martin back by dinner time." And with that, he slapped the reins and sending the mules down to the road towards Nightshade.

Star shouted to them as they left. "See you folks at dinner then," She laughed to herself, "the man don't even know what's happening to him"

The morning was cool and comfortable. The first week in August, mornings were pleasant. But late afternoon, it was hot, not unbearable but enough to stay outdoors in the shade when possible. She half wished she should have stayed to go swimming with Jacob.

Riding beside Sam was something different. Usually, there was Jacob between them. Now it was only her and a little dead space instead. As the mules slowly walked the dirt highway, she nervously tried to strike up conversation with Sam.

"So, do you have to get a lot of supplies Mr. Anderson?"

"Well now, Mrs. Martin you made the list, so you should know how much we need."

"Oh of course. I just thought you might have something else other than what I needed."

"Nope, just the same."

"Uhm Mr. Anderson, do you think that its' going to be a long summer this year?"

"Likely to be."

"Mr. Anderson do you like summer or spring better?"

What? He was puzzled about the inane questioning.

"One's about the same as another to me."

"Mr. Anderson, do you have a favorite color?"

Sam pulled back on the reins, the mules coming to an abrupt stop. He turned to Hannah.

"Are you feelin' well Mrs. Martin? You seem to be fidgety for some reason. What color do I like? What kind of conversation is that? If there's somethin' on your mind, spit it out."

"I ah, I ah, I wanted to invite you to Jacob's birthday party next Saturday. It's going to be a picnic outside the quarters house. You don't have to bring anything. I'll take care of it all. He's going to be ten and I know he would love to have you come, He thinks so much of you. And there will be the Lowoods and my cousin and.......

"Now hold on a minute. You mean to tell me you been hem hawin' around to ask me to go to a kid birthday party? Is this how you figured it to be? You trap me on the way to town to get me to agree to go to a birthday party? In your house. That house, the house that I.... He mumbled something that Hannah wasn't able to hear. You tryin' to pull one over on me? Why I expected better of you Mrs. Martin. You shouldn't......

As his voice trailed off Hannah felt her face get hot. Trap him? Trap him? How dare he. Who did he think he was? Was he really that arrogant? Stupid? Her frustration was building with every word coming from his mouth. As he continued to rant. Hannah's her ears began filling with indignant steam. He was forming words, but they weren't making sense. He should stop. Stop talking. Stop with the accusations and insinuations, just stop it. And before she realized what she was doing, she had his face between her hands, pulling him close to her, kissing him forcefully. So forcefully, his hat fell off his head onto the floor of the buckboard.

Shocked, Sam's eyes opened wide. What happened? And while he was going through these emotions, Hannah, (in shock herself) moved out of frustration gear and shifted into uh oh gear. Sam pulled himself away slowly, sitting up straight, staring at her, face to face.

"Oh. Ohh. Oh Mr. Anderson, I'm so so sorry. I didn't mean to do that. I just, I mean. Please, forgive me. I can't tell you how sorry I am that happened. I don't know what came over me. I just got a little upset about you thinking I would trap you. Believe me, the only thing I wanted was to have you come to Jacob's birthday party. I knew you still had some feelings about the house. I just wasn't sure how you felt about coming over for a party. I should have gone about it in a better way. I hope you don't hold this against me."

Stumbling for words he, tried reconnecting to clarity, and it was taking him a bit to make that connection. His eyes went to the buckboard floor, seeing that somehow, he lost his hat. He reached down to the buckboard floor to retrieve it, at the same time Hannah was already bending down to do the same, they awkwardly butted each other's heads. She reached the hat before he did and sheepishly handed it to him. Instead of putting it back on his head, he held it between his hands and fiddled with the brim for a minute to collect his bearings.

"Oh, sorry again Mr. Anderson I'm so sorry."

He managed to recover himself offering a bland response.

"Umm, okay then. Well, no harm done. Let's be on our way, we have things to get done."

Sam stuffed the hat, hard down on his head. He clicked to the mules focusing his attention on getting to town as quickly as possible. The awkwardness of the silence between them the rest of the way was palpable. They arrived in Nightshade, the sun now beaming down on them both. A clear blue sky met them as they pulled into town. Quite the opposite of the storm that was brewing inside of Sam Anderson and Hannah Martin.

# CHAPTER 48

Hannah was glad when they pulled into Nightshade. She was ready to get out of the wagon as soon as possible. It had been torture riding next to him. She conceded to the walled silence. Kiss him? What in the world was that? Emotions had overridden her sensibility. Patience and humility were sacrificed impetuously. Thank goodness the Lord is merciful. The riling's of an obstinate man shook her secure space. The space inside that kept her grounded to reason.

He'd been thrown off balance, kissing him that way. If he hadn't overreacted things might not have gotten so out of hand. Accusing her of trapping him? What was it about him and that house? After all these years, what could still be bothering him?

Kissing him did shut him up, though probably not the smart thing to do. She admitted to herself that she was caught up in the heat of the moment. She was truly sorry to put him in an embarrassing position. The overwhelming power to kiss him was wrong. Too powerful. Scary powerful.

Hannah climbed down from the wagon, as Sam hitched the team to the post in front of the general store.

"So, mam, are ya hungry? We could eat some breakfast before we start the day."

Solemnly, she answered, "Yes Mr. Anderson, that would be nice, sort of a peace meal?"

"Mrs. Martin, I might've been a little out of sorts about the invite. He scratched his head. Not sure how it got to where it went, but if you pardon my actions, I'll pardon yours."

"Sounds fair to me Mr. Anderson. Lead on. I'll pay for my own breakfast if it's all the same."

"Well now mam, I admit I'm a stubborn man, but I'd never dishonor the manners my mama raised me with."

"I sure wouldn't want you to have to dishonor your mama. I'd be obliged then."

They walked into the café of the Royal Inn, the waitress on duty, greeting them with a cheery good morning. She led them to a table in front of a window facing the street. The tables were covered with white cotton tablecloths and fancy silverware wrapped in linen napkins. There were only a few patrons in the café for the morning. Sam asked the waitress to bring them coffee as she handed the menus. "For you both sir?" He nodded to confirm. She then left them to themselves to decide their order.

"What's good Mr. Anderson?"

"Can't go wrong with much of anything. Typical breakfast things like, ham eggs, biscuit, toast. It's all tasty. Take your pick."

After a few minutes the waitress returned with cups and a coffee kettle, then took their orders down on her notepad before disappearing off to turn it over to the cook.

"Mr. Anderson? I don't want to step on your toes again, and if you need time to answer about coming to Jacob's birthday party, please feel free to study on it."

'Sam took a slow sip of his coffee, he peered into the cup, responding to her without even looking up.

"You're not gonna kiss me again are ya Miss Martin? I'm afraid if I say no, it may get a little embarrasin' here in this public place."

Hannah blushed. She was thankful at least he was being gracious about it all.

"Oh, now Mr. Anderson. Don't tease. I feel bad about it. It won't happen again. I just think you'd find yourself having a nice time. It'd be good for you to be around friends and neighbors. I know Jacob would love to have you there."

"You don't wanna consider havin' the party at the main house? It might be more comfortable for folks."

"Thank you for offering, but Jacob loves his room and living at the quarters. He's so proud to have his friends over. It's going to be a picnic outdoors as long as the weather is nice."

"Picnic? Well, I might consider it. Give me time to think about it. Nothin' against you or the boy, I just have to work some things out in my head pertainin' to some history of that old house. It just takes time to get used to."

"If I'm not being too personal, do you mind if I ask what you mean by that?"

"Well now mam, I think you crossed that personal line earlier this mornin'. Mrs. Martin. I'll tell ya, when I built that house, it was meant as a gift for my bride. I spent a lot of time and hard sweat building that house with my father to make things right for her. It came down a few days after it was built and just a day before we were to occupy it as man and wife, she changed her mind. I can't look at that house without gettin' a bad feelin.' It didn't get any better when my friend Tom wound up dyin' there. So, ya see, anything havin' to do with bein' around that house comes with bad memories. A person can build up a lifetime of hardness in his heart with memories like that."

"I didn't know Mr. Anderson. I'm sorry. I do understand. I can't blame you feeling the way you do about it. But do you think you'll always feel that way? I think you might change your mind if you those memories could be exchanged for new and good ones. Such as spending time with friends and neighbors to celebrate a little boy's birthday."

Sam paused a moment. Looking at her face right then, he saw a kindness in her eyes which brought him back a moment to how different her face looked before she kissed him. He wondered how it might have felt, had she not been frustrated with him.

I'll tell ya what." Sam took a last sip from his coffee cup before setting on the table." For now, let's say I'll give it a thought. We'll leave it as a maybe. But if I change my mind, alls I ask is that you don't hold it to me."

"That's fair. It's a start. We'll leave it at maybe yes then."

Just then the waitress brought their food, asking them if they needed anything else. Hannah bowed her head. Sam followed suit. He seemed more at ease. As he bowed his head, this time she saw him close his eyes.

"Thank, you Lord for this thy bounty and asking for your generous mercy for anything causing dishonor to your name. Amen."

Not sure if Sam understood the meaning of it, nonetheless she was sure the Lord did.

They finished their meal with Hannah explaining how she wound up in Nightshade. She told him about Jack's death, how Naomi offered to take her and Jacob in, and how she came to answer the help wanted ad. Sam was curious as to what brought her there. It must have been difficult for her moving all alone away from home. She was a strong woman, he had to give her that.

The conversation drifted back to Jacob's birthday.

"Mr. Anderson I was wondering if you would mind helping me pick out a pair of cowboy boots and a hat for Jacob. He wears a size nine in shoes and I'm not quite sure about a hat. Do you think you could help me?"

"I'd be okay with that. By the way, Mrs. Martin. Since we are bein' a little personal here, and I do mean that in every sense of the word, you mind callin' me Sam instead of mister? It just seems more reasonable."

"Only if you call me Hannah. Your right its reasonable."

And in a rare moment she saw his face change from grim into a broad smile. And a nice face it was.

# CHAPTER 49

Breakfast was over. Sam and Hannah walked out to the street discussing plans for the day.

"I have to go to the post office and check in with Mr. Barney, Hannah. I'd kinda like to visit Grover at the newspaper. Then I'll be gettin' over to the general store. You can do your shoppin' while I'm busy with that. We can meet up there later if ya want. I'll take a good look at the boots and hats. You may need to guide me on what ya think he'll like."

"Thank you, Mr. Anderson, Um Sam. I do have a few things I need to get myself, a few sundries and such. How long do you think you'll be?"

"Oh, not much more than an hour. I'd guess. If I get done before hand, I'll come lookin' for ya. Shouldn't be too hard to find you in this little town."

"Sounds good. And if you're still busy when I'm done, I'll come looking for you."

Sam tipped his hat," all right mam, See ya soon then."

She watched him walk down the wood sidewalks towards the post office. My what a proud hulk of a man he was. Maybe Star was right could be the Lord was using her to help break down those walls. For whatever reason he had for putting her in this place at this time, she just had to keep faith. An imperfect faith maybe, but time would thresh it out. Things might just work out for something good, good for the both of them.

# CHAPTER 50

Hannah stopped in at the apothecary to pick up some cooking spices and a bottle of rose oil perfume. She loved the smell of rose oil. It reminded her of when she was a child when her mother would sprinkle it in the bath water. Back then a bath was just a tin tub. Bathwater shared by brothers and sisters. Now in the quarters there was a lovely porcelain claw tub to bathe in. Adding a kettle of boiling water helped to bring it to a comfortable temperature. With the warm days of summer in place, boiling water was added less and less. She looked forward to taking a long bath in the rose oil. Of course she had to wait until Jacob was asleep to soak, that wouldn't be until later. For now, she needed to get on with the purpose of the day.

Hannah found the dress shop open, with her being the only customer this early in the day. She was introduced to the two sisters that ran the shop, Ms. Sarah Hutchins and her married sister, Sally Frances.

The sisters welcomed her with broad smiles escorting her in the direction of a row of racks filled with new dresses that just arrived in from Little Rock.

"Is this for a special occasion Mrs. Martin?" Sally searched through the new batch of dresses searching for what she thought would be an appropriate match.

"Well, I was thinking that I would like something that would do for an outside party. Nothing too dressy but not plain either. And I'd like a new bonnet to match."

"We have a few dresses you might be interested in. There's a dressing room in the back and here is a full mirror for you to see how it looks." Sarah motioned to a long slender mirror standing upright by the wall.

She looked over the various dresses, stopping a few times to look at a blue oval crinoline with a full bustle, then onto a lavender dress with sloping sleeves. She liked the lavender; it would show off her slender arms and neck.

She pulled them off the rack, lifting them up for the sisters to see.

"May I try these two?"

"Of course. Those will look lovely on you. Sally, show Mrs. Martin to the dressing room and then help her with the bustle if she needs it. Will you need a corset with those Mrs. Martin? We have a sale on our longline brands, they help define the hips and bustline."

Hannah thought about that for a moment. She did need a little help in both of those areas.

"Yes, that sounds fine. I'll just see what it looks like with and without one before I make up my mind. Thank you."

She was assisted to the dressing room by Sally holding an arm full of dresses, bonnets and a wire corset. Nothing like a new dress to make a woman feel right.

# CHAPTER 51

Sam had only a few things to pick up at the post office. Mr. Barney handed him a post card stamped from Kansas. It was from Serita. He read the card as he walked out of the post office. She was getting on well it said. She and her sister were enjoying spending time cooking, gossiping and catching up on each other's affairs. She wondered how Sam was getting along and if he had a new housekeeper yet. Sam chuckled to himself thinking how Serita would be surprised if she saw what was going on at the ranch now. He'd have Hannah write her back. Sure, was a lot of changin' goin'on. He hadn't expected so much change. Some for the good, some for the better. He thanked Mr. Barney waving to him as he walked over to stop in on Grover at the newspaper. He just wanted to catch up on events since the last time they spoke.

He found Grover reading a copy of the newest edition of the Nightshade Editor. Grover put down the paper and made his way over to shake hands.

"Well, hello there Sam, I was wonderin' about you. How's the housekeeper workin' out?"

"I'd say about as best as could be expected. She ain't no Serita but she sets a fine table and I'm pleased with it."

They talked briefly about Nightshade politics before Sam pulled out his watch to check the time.

"

"Speakin' of the housekeeper, I need to be headin' off to meet up with her. She had a little shoppin' business to do in town, so I need to be gettin' along to see if she's ready to head back."

"You and her alone together Sam? I'm a little surprised to hear that. She must've had a powerful need for shoppin' if she rode in alone with you." Grover chuckled a little.

"Nothin' to it Grover. I was comin' to town anyway for supplies and she just tagged along. I'd better be goin'. It was good to see you again."

. Hannah mentioned she had to pick up sundries, so he stopped at the apothecary first. The druggist told him she'd already left and appeared to be headed towards the dress shop. Dress shop? She didn't say anything to him about it. He knew of it. The same shop where he first saw Amelia. Sam shifted his thoughts back to Serita's post card, rereading it as he ambled along down the wooden sidewalk right up until he found himself standing in front of the window of Nightshade Dress and Petticoat.

# CHAPTER 52

Sally Frances helped Hannah pull the corset then steadied the bustle while she stepped in. She slipped the blue crinoline over Hannah's head and slid it down over the corset first, then bustle. As she pulled the dress in place Hannah felt the fabric against her skin. It was silky smooth, it felt so soft she didn't mind the discomfort of the corset. She'd try the bonnet on later. For now, she was curious to see how the dress fit.

Sally lifted up on the bustle as she followed Hannah out to the mirror. When Hannah saw herself, she was surprised how much she had changed from a year ago. She thought her color seemed a little brighter than before. Could be the dress. She didn't seem as pale or drab than when she first moved in with Naomi. Sadness does a lot to a body. She had to admit the years of worry had taken a toll on her. Not so bad now seeing herself in this dress. She twisted to each side to see what it looked like in motion.

Sam had been going over Serita's post card as he stopped in front of the dress shop. He was turning the post card over to read Serita's address. He happened to look up as Hannah stood at the mirror looking at herself in a new dress. She didn't notice him at first. She was too intent on admiring the way fabric moved. Sam stared through the window. He was captured by the way her long shiny hair draped over her shoulders, thinking to himself that her eyes were almost as blue as the dress she was wearing. Seeing her in that dress was, well, it was mesmerizing. He thought back to the day he was with her and Jacob, at top of the ridge, looking out over the rolling hills of the Triple S. The same feeling of peacefulness and happiness, Happiness. That was new. But it hadn't dawned on him, this was the very same window and store that he first saw Amelia.

Hannah didn't know how long Sam had been standing there before she saw him. He was staring. She pretended not to see him and went on turning from one side to the other, keeping her attention to the mirror with one eye and peeking at him with the other. So, Sam Anderson, could be there was a crack in that wall of yours.

Sally Frances was the first sister to see him.

"Oh, Mrs. Martin, is this someone you know? I believe he approves of the dress you're wearing."

"That's Sam Anderson. I work for him. I'll take this and the lavender dress. Ms. Frances. You can wrap up those bonnets and the corset too. Please tell him, Mr. Anderson, to come in and wait while I change back into my clothes. He looks a little uncomfortable standing out there."

Ms. Sarah waved for Sam to come to the door while Sally and Hannah returned to the dressing room to change,

"Mr. Anderson? I'm Sarah, that's my sister Sally. Please come in. Mrs. Martin was just finishing up. Do you approve of her new dress? She looks awfully pretty in it."

Sam removed his hat, hanging his head a bit, realizing he'd been caught gawking.

"Nice to meet ya mam. I ah, I think if she approves of it, I wouldn't disagree with it. Will she be long? We gotta a few more things to take care of before leavin' town this mornin.'"

"You just wait here sir; she's changing and shouldn't be long at all."

Hannah returned holding two boxes of new clothes.

"Thank you both ladies, it's been an eventful day. I'm sure I'll be back again sometime to see what other things I can look over." She paid the sisters for the dresses and gathered up the boxes.

"Let me take those for you Hannah. I'll just put them in the buckboard while we're gettin' supplies."

"So, what did you think?"

"What did I think about what?"

"You saw me in the window, didn't you? What did you think about the dress?"

"Now you're teasin' me aren't you? I guess I deserve that after all I've said and done."

"Don't change the subject, what did you think?"

"I think we need to be gettin' over to the general to get supplies and Jacob's birthday present."

She laughed. He didn't need to answer. She knew exactly what he thought, and the ride home would be interesting to say the least.

# CHAPTER 53

Sam settled on a pair of black shiny cowboy boots with a matching black hat for Jacob. Hannah was satisfied with his choice, agreeing that Jacob needed a larger size of boots to have room to grow into.

Sam packed away all the supplies in back but kept Hannah's dresses and, Jacob's new duds situated between him and Hannah up front. She rearranged the packages in a tidy heap, allowing more room for her to sit closer to Sam. He didn't seem to notice.

"If you'd like we can drop off the supplies and put Jacob's things at the main house before goin' on to the Lowoods. That way it'd be a surprise for 'em before his birthday."

"Why that's a lovely suggestion Sam, I believe we'll do just that, thank you."

The time back to the Triple S passed smoothly. They were both a little tired, so conversation was minimal. It was a nice feeling for Sam, her bein' next to him. He still wasn't too keen on the idea of goin' to the party. But he had told Hannah he would think about it. He had to ride fences again tomorrow. That's the best time for serious thinkin' on the back of a horse lookin' out over the ridge.

As they pulled up to the main house Hannah helped him unload the buckboard, putting supplies up, along with Jacob's new clothes. Then back to the Lowoods to fetch Jacob.

Jacob saw them coming up the path. He and Gennie were playing on the tree swing. It had been a fun day for him. The Lowoods boys showed him how to catch tadpoles, letting them loose back into the creek after each wiggly froglet slipped through his fingers. Gennie didn't like the slime of them, so she waded in the creek with her dress hiked up above her bare ankles while the boys fished around for more tadpoles. He loved to swing out on the tree rope falling in the creek just as it reached the water. Gennie laughed at them when Luke and John swung out on the rope together falling over each other in the water.

Jacob thought what it would have been like if he'd had a brother. They sure did seem to have fun with each other.

Star was sitting on the porch enjoying watching Gennie and Jacob play. The buckboard was just then coming down the dirt path, Hannah was seated closer to Sam, closer than when she saw them leaving that morning. She wondered if Hannah had talked him into going to the party. By the looks of it, it was a good chance.

"Jacob come on an get your things ready, your mama's here to get you."

"Yes mam. Come on Gennie, I'll race you to the house." They took off together, both barefooted reaching the porch at the same time.

"Well now, did you both get your chores done in town today? Seems like you made it back without too much trouble."

"We got a lot accomplished today, Star, Sam and I are ready to get Jacob back so we can get dinner ready. Speaking of trouble, I hope he wasn't too much for you."

"Oh no, he fit in just fine with the other ones. Gennie and he have been playing hard today so I bet they sleep well tonight. Sam now is it then? Well, looks like that trip to town did a lot for the name calling situation."

Sam scowled at Star," Don't go diggin' around for bones Star."

She waved him off, laughing quietly. "I was just making known an obvious fact."

"We just thought it would be reasonable to call each other by name from now on. There's really nothing special to it."

Hannah changed the subject to avoid any further embarrassment over the matter.

"Thanks for keeping Jacob, Star. I think I have everything I need for the birthday party in two weeks. Jacob has been excited knowing that Gennie and the boys will be there. I'm looking forward to it myself

# CHAPTER 54

Star and family showed up early to the quarters to help Hannah get the party ready. They brought two picnic tables that Alvin and the boys put together. Star brought cold fried chicken and potato salad with her. Hannah baked the cake and yeast rolls. She was in the kitchen talking to Naomi, while they were cutting lemons up to make lemonade.

"So, is Mr. Anderson going to be here Hannah? He'll miss a lot of good food if he doesn't come."

"He's been pretty quiet about it. We'll, just have to wait and see. While I was at the house yesterday to get Jacob's presents, he didn't say much to me. Actually, he's been quiet ever since we came back from Nightshade. We'll just go on with or without him."

Star came in from outside, "Hannah, Alvin fixed up a wood swing for Jacob's present, where will you want him to put it when it's time?"

"Star that is a thoughtful gift, I'll have to thank Alvin. I think we'll put it up on that old sycamore in front. It's sturdy enough and perfect for a swing." Naomi and I are almost done in here, we were just talking about whether Sam is coming. You wouldn't know about it would you?"

"He's a private man Hannah, even with Alvin, he don't say much about how he's thinking. Though Alvin seems to think there's been something bothering him."

"We ought to be getting ready Hannah, those kids are getting a little rowdy outside. Star is there anything you need help with? Everything is done in here so I can round up everybody to eat."

"I think we're ready Ms. Naomi. Alvin and the boys can help with anything else that needs heavy lifting. Well, let's have a party."

Gennie, Jacob and Naomi's girls were running around chasing chickens off the porch. Hannah hoped Sam would be there to see what happiness looks and sounds like. She guessed he decided it was too much for him to deal with.

Everyone sat down together at the tables. Hannah stood up to say a few words before asking the blessing.

"I want to thank everyone for being here for Jacob on his special day. He's ten years old today. I know he is happy for you all sharing his birthday. Right Jacob?"

"Yes mam. Thanks everybody!"

"All right. Would everyone please bow their heads?"

As she closed her eyes, she heard the sound of horse steps getting nearer. And then she opened her eyes and saw him. He stopped Skip at the sycamore tree swung out of the saddle and hitched him to a low branch. Sam took his hat off hanging it on the saddle horn. In his hands he held what looked like a book wrapped up in butcher paper.

"I hope I didn't get here too late. I was busy tryin' to decide which present I could bring. So, I just brought both of them."

"No, you're just in time for the blessing. We're glad you could come." Hannah was glad to see him.

"Mr. Anderson, could I ride Skip later? That's the only present I want."

"Now Jacob, don't you be so bold. Mr. Anderson is kind enough to come to your party, don't start making demands on him before he even sits to eat,"

"It's okay mam, I think we can arrange for Skip to give Mr. Jacob and the others a ride. That is as long as you're fine with it."

"Sam, I haven't seen you wear that shirt before, is that new?"

"Alvin, I have a few good shirts I pull out on special occasions. Ya got anythin' against that?"

"You look fine Mr. Anderson, come on and sit down, we are all happy you came."

"Thank you, Ms. Naomi, good seein' you folks again. Nice to meet you Mr. Sanders."

"Call me Robert, Mr. Anderson. I'm sorry I didn't get to meet you the day you came to the house. I was in the office doing dental work on some people."

"Sam, to ya, Robert. I figured it was you because I saw you with your family in pictures on the wall that day.

"It's nice to meet you too. Sam." Robert held his hand out to return a handshake.

Sam made his way to the table, choosing to take a seat next to Jacob and in between Hannah and Naomi.

"Let's start over now. Dear Lord, thank you for this lovely day to celebrate Jacob Martin's tenth birthday. We are thankful for friends and family gathered here at this table to honor you in providing us with this bounty. Let us always remember what you do for us from sunrise to sundown, day and night, in stormy weather or sunny skies. Thank you for bringing Jacob and I to this place we call home. In the name of your son Amen."

# CHAPTER 55

"Can I open my presents now mama? Looks like everybody is done eating."

"You are a little feisty today son. But it's your day so if everyone is ready, I think we can go ahead."

"First the Lowoods made you a special gift, I think you're gonna be happy with."

"Jacob, me and the boys seen how you and Gennie love to swing, so we made you this for your own self. We'll go ahead and string it up on a tree and it'll be ready in just a bit."

"Thank you Mr. Lowoods."

"Jacob since Skip is tied to the tree your swing is goin 'on, how bout you and the other kids get a ride on ole Skip while Alvin is settin' it up?"

"Is it okay mama?"

Hannah laughed," Okay go on, but you let Gennie and your cousins go first. You don't get to forget your manners just because it's your birthday."

While the men, boys and girls were all busy with the new swing and riding Skip, Hannah sat with Naomi and Star to talk about the surprise of Sam showing up.

"Hannah, he had to be nervous about coming. There must be some major reason for him to be able to be here seeing he had to face up to the ghosts of this house."

"Star, I know it has been hard on him. I just think it's time for him to face those old ghosts once and for all. It was his decision. He wasn't pressured into coming today. That says a lot about the man he is. I'm very proud of him."

"Hannah just be careful; a wounded man can be unpredictable. I would take my time trying to make any changes in him, you have to remember what it was like with Jack. You lived with a wounded man for a long time. Make sure you don't; go down that road again."

"I'm not taking anything for granted Naomi, I just let the Lord use me for whatever is needed to help Sam find his way. He's not like Jack, nor would I want him to be. I just know he needs a little help, and if the Lord's willing I'm willing."

Sam lifted Gennie and Naomi's girls up to the saddle, walking all three of them around the yard. They squealed with delight when Skip tossed his head, flicking his mane onto them. After a few rounds, he set each girl down, they ran off to check out the swing Alvin had put up. Jacob waited patiently for his turn.

"Mr. Anderson, could I try and ride Skip on my own, I know how to work the reins and you can be right by me to help if I need it,"

"I think that might be all right. Okay, but you do what I say and don't you try and make Skip trot."

Sam lifted up Jacob and handed him the reins. He clicked to Skip, just like he had seen Sam do many times before. Jacob walked Skip around the yard and up to the tables where Hannah, Naomi, and Star were seated.

"Look mama, I can ride all by myself. See. Mr. Anderson says I'm doing good. See me Ms. Naomi, Ms. Star."

"You better not get too big for your britches son; Mr. Anderson may need to teach you a little bit about being humble instead. Don't take too long. There are a few more gifts for you so get on down and call the girls over to eat cake."

"Gotta listen to your ma, son. Let's give Skip a break so's you can get on with the presents."

"Here you go Jacob, this is from me, your Uncle Robert, Lizzy and Jane, Happy birthday!"

Naomi handed him a picnic basket filled with cookies and rock candy.

"Now son, you take it easy with this, I don't want to have to treat a rotten tooth come soon. Just a piece a day, okay? Moderation. All in moderation."

"Thank you, Uncle Robert, is it okay if I share it with everyone now?"

"Sounds like a fine thing to do Jacob."

"Jacob, I have a present for you. I hope you like it. Mr. Anderson helped pick it out for you."

Hannah handed him a parcel with the boots and hat inside. He opened it with a giant-sized smile attached.

"I've been waiting on this since last Christmas mama."

He immediately shucked his old brown leather lace ups off, exchanging them for the new boots. It was a little tricky at first, but he managed to keep his balance, eventually making a trip around the picnic table without falling. Once he got the hang of the boots he put on the hat, making the outfit complete.

"I'm a real cowboy now, just like Mr. Anderson."

"Well now Jacob, I have a present or two for you. Here ya go."

Sam handed him the butcher papered gift then reached in his pocket to offer him the old pocketknife he purchased when he lost his old one.

Jacob took the knife from him, whistling a shrill noise through his teeth. He turned it overlooking intently at it, admiring the blade with the eagle's wing.

"By goodness, that is a dandy knife, Mr. Anderson, I couldn't think of a better present than this."

"Well here's somethin' else for ya, It's a book about Robinson Crusoe. It was one of my favorites, I hope you enjoy it. It's yours to keep."

"Hey Gennie, come look at the book Mr. Anderson gave me." He ran over to Gennie and the Sanders girls to show them the knife and book.

"I'm sorry Sam, he seems to have forgotten his manners."

"No harm done Hannah, but it looks like he forgot about the most important thing... cake."

"Jacob, you and the girls come on now, everybody is waiting to eat birthday cake. You can show everyone your presents after cake."

All the Lowoods, the Sanders, Sam and Hannah gathered round the picnic table and sang happy birthday to the happiest ten-year-old in the whole state of Arkansas.

# CHAPTER 56

Everyone left back to their own homes after eating cake and visiting each other, finishing the day from Jacob's party. Naomi and Star helped Hannah clean up before leaving home. Hannah and Sam were left by themselves, sitting alone at the picnic table. Jacob was trying out his new swing, still wearing his cowboy hat and new boots.

"I'm happy you were here today, Sam, to tell the truth, I really didn't expect you to be here."

"I thought on it long and hard. I thought about how you said, sometimes you can replace old hard memories with new, better ones. So, well, I said to myself, Sam Anderson, there might be somethin' to that notion. I'm not one to keep bangin' my head against the wall, expectin' the wall to break and not my head. So that's how I found myself here today, in a place that I swore twenty years ago I wouldn't be in. Ya know, it's a little your fault for that."

"What do you mean, my fault?" I didn't force you to come. You're the one that chose to keep "bangin your head', It's not my head that's banging on a wall. I just thought you'd needed a break from the head banging."

"Now I know what you're sayin' makes sense, you bein' a woman might not understand that a man has his pride. I lost a little bit of that when Amelia left. It's taken me a long time to figure out that this house wasn't the cause of it, it just was a reminder of it. I have to thank you for showin' me that's all this house is, a reminder not a curse."

Hannah could see he was still dealing with a broken heart, at least he was starting to work his way into forgiveness from the past.

"Sam, I do understand. I lived with a man that had his own demons. He died before he could get past it. But you have a chance to move on from it. I pray for you every night that the Lord will show you how to forgive. I'm sorry about Amelia, she was wrong for what she did to you. You shouldn't keep blaming her for it. There are people that care about you. Here and now. I care about you. You're a fine man. Yes, you're stubborn and hard to get along with. But I see how you are with Jacob, how you are with Star and Alvin. I know how you were with Tom and Serita. There is hope for you Sam."

"Mama, can I have a piece of candy. I only ate one little piece." Jacob jumped from the swing and shouted his request to Hannah. He could see that she and Mr. Anderson were in some sort of serious talk.

"Just one more little piece Jacob. Mr. Anderson and I were just talking about you. Come on. We'll all eat a little piece. How bout you Mr. Anderson, care for a piece of salt taffy? Naomi has the best in the county."

Sam was glad for a change in conversation. "Sure thing, nothin' like a good ole piece of taffy to end the day."

# CHAPTER 57

It was getting to be late fall. The days were getting shorter, and Hannah felt a chill in the air. She was up early to read her Bible. She read out loud the verse in James where he encourages believers to humble themselves before the Lord and he will lift you up. God opposes the proud but gives grace to the humble. She prayed that she would be an example of humbleness by living out the promise of grace. The Lord had blessed her with good friends and family. She admitted that having Sam in her life made it difficult at times to remain humble. Maybe it was all part of the plan. She prayed so many times Sam would see that the Lord wasn't against him, far from it. He just needed to know that.

She started to wake Jacob up to go collect the eggs, but he was all cuddled up in bed, looking so sweet, she didn't have the heart to disturb him. For this morning, she would take care of it and let him sleep in a little longer. She pulled on her cotton housecoat, wrapped its cloth belt tight around her waist and slipped into her shoes, ready to start the morning.

The hens were beginning to lay less these days. With the daylight hours getting less and less they were getting half the amount than from a few short weeks ago. She headed out to the coup, the rooster already up and crowing to his flock. She stepped inside the coop, the hens, a little unsettled, moved from their nests, jumping down to sneak past her on their way out to forage for bugs. The eggs were piled in a heap, still slightly warm from being recently laid. As she pulled each one to place in the basket, she felt a sharp sting. Thinking it was only a burr in the hay, she saw a slithery tail emerge from underneath the egg pile. Instantly, she knew she had to act quickly. Hannah pulled away the belt of her housecoat wrapping it around her arm, tying it as tightly as she could manage to get it. She had to send for help, being aware that any fast movement could send poison deeper into her body. Hannah walked slowly back to the house, holding her arm next to her chest. She shook Jacob firmly pulling him up from the bed.

"Jacob! Jacob!, Get up, wake up Jacob!" He moved sluggishly at the sound of her voice. He was confused, did he do something wrong?

"Jacob!"

"Yes mam? Did I over sleep mama?"

"Jacob, Listen to me very carefully. I want you to remember word for word what I'm about to tell you. Word for word you hear me? You run as fast as you can to the main house and get Mr. Anderson. Tell him that your mama had some trouble in the hen house this morning and that he must come right away. Tell him your mama needs him urgently. Can you do that?

"What's wrong mama?"

"There's no time for questions, you go on and say exactly how I told you. Tell Mr. Anderson I'll be down by the spring cellar and he's not to dawdle. You go on now, you understand?"

'Yes mam, I'll tell him."

He ran out of the screen door, still wearing his nightgown. Hannah watched him, thinking she was glad she was the one who got the eggs this morning, instead of Jacob. The Lord had protected him. She was beginning to feel flushed, she made her way from the house, making it down to the spring just as the sun shone through the clouds, she laid down in the cold water still keeping her arm held tightly to her chest. And before she closed her eyes, she thanked the Lord for sparing little Jacob.

# CHAPTER 58

Sam woke up early, drinking his coffee in the barn as he walked Sable out for her morning brush down. She was tied up to the stall door when he noticed her ears had perked up to something. Her eyes were fixed on the open barn door. That's when Sam heard what sounded like Jacob calling his name. He put down the brush and walked to the door to see what was going on. Jacob was screaming loudly, barefooted and still wearing his nightclothes,

"Jacob, I'm here in the barn with Sable. What's the meanin' of this with you still in your nightgown?"

"Mr. Anderson, Mr. Anderson, you gotta come quick. My mama told me to tell you she had trouble in the chicken coup this morning. She said for you to not dawdle that she needs you to come right this minute!"

It didn't take Sam long to figure out what happened. He slung a rope over Sable, grabbed Jacob, throwing him over her bareback. Then he jumped on while kicking Sable, jolting the both of them forward.

"You hang on now son, I'm gonna need your help. Where's your mama at?"

"She said to tell you she would be down at the spring cellar."

They pulled up to the front porch, Sam jumping off before Sable came to a full stop.

"Now Jacob, son, I need you to do me a favor, you ride ole Sable here as fast as you can go, and you get Ms. Star and Mr. Alvin. You tell them, that your mama is very sick, and she needs them to come help. I want you to stay there with Gennie and the boys until I come for you, you hear me? It might be a while but I promise I'll come back to get you when your mama feels better."

"What's wrong with her Mr. Anderson?"

"Well, she's gonna be fine Jacob, she's just don't feel very well right now. Now you go on, you gotta hurry it up. Hang on tight boy!""

And with that he slapped Sable on the rear, causing her to leap out with Jacob holding on for dear life.

Sam ran down to the spring creek and was terrified in what he saw. Hannah laying on her back in the water, eyes closed still in her nightclothes. Her hand was clutched to her chest with the tie of her housecoat wrapped around her arm. It was swollen and bright red. He bent down to try to rouse her, but she only moaned softly. He pulled her from the creek water, lifting her body up as he carried her, running as fast as he could back to the house. Once inside, he removed her wet clothes ensuring the tie from her housecoat was still in place. He pulled all the blankets out of the closet and wrapped them around her as he laid her down on the bed. Then he set a fire in the fireplace with old kindling wood that was left over from winter and hung her wet clothes up over the mantel to dry them out. Her skin was so cold, and she was so still. He felt helpless. The sound of Star and Alvin shouting through the screen door was a welcome comfort for the moment.

"Sam, Sam! What in the world has happened? Jacob looked like he saw a ghost. I knew it was something bad when I saw him riding up alone on Sable."

"It's Hannah, Alvin. I think she got snake bit in the chicken coop this mornin'. I found her down in the creek with her housecoat belt tied around her arm. Looks like it got her on the hand. It's pretty swollen and she is breathin' but just barely. I didn't think Doc Turner could get here fast enough, but I know Star knows Indian medicine so I figured maybe she could help her until doc can get here,"

"She looks pretty bad Sam. Alvin you go on and fetch Doc Turner. I'll stay here with Hannah and try to fix up a poultice until you get back."

"Good enough. I'll be praying on my way that the Lord has his hand on her. You go on Star; you help Ms. Hannah."

Alvin kissed her then and ran out to jump in the wagon, slapping the team of mules with the leather reins.

"I'm gonna need some of your horse liniment, some old coffee grounds, whisky, and cocklebur. Find a sharp knife and cut up some cotton sheets for bandages. You'll have to boil them in hot water first. While you're getting all that, I'm gonna to draw some water and try to get her to drink. If we caught it early, she should be all right until Alvin gets back with Doc Turner."

Star could see the worried look on Sam's face. His eyes were filled with concern and held back tears. Poor Sam. She would do her best to help both of them. "You've done your best for her, Sam. It's left up to her and the good Lord now. Keep your hopes up. She's a tough lady." Sam knew that all too well.

# CHAPTER 59

Doc Turner arrived just after Star had applied the bandages to Hannah's arm. She made a little incision in the cut below the tied housecoat belt, applying the poultice to the wound, then wrapping it with the hot bandages that Sam had cut.

"I don't know Star. The poultice may help, just hope the poison hasn't gotten too far in her system. All we can do now is just wait and see. I'll give her an injection for pain and one to slow her heartrate down, maybe it will slow the venom and give her a chance for her body to fight it. She's young and healthy. She's got every chance in the world going for her. We should know better within the next twenty-four hours if it's going to work. Probably need to take shifts changing those bandages though. Every three hours or so, they'll need to be refreshed."

"You think she'll pull through Doc?"

"Well Sam, it's hard to say. She helped herself with that homemade ligature and gettin in cold water at the creek. Pretty smart thinkin'. That right there helped slow down the venom. She's going to need time and a little help from above, Star and I will do our best. Don't; you fret son. She's fighting it and that's half the battle. I have to leave for a little bit to go check on Ms. Lancet. She's due a baby any day and I need to take a look at her. She lost a baby last summer so I'm watching her pretty close these last few days. I'll stop back by and see how Ms. Hannah is getting along. Star and Alvin can take care of her until I get back. You just keep your hopes up there now, Sam."

He shook Doc Turner's hand and thanked him for helping

Hannah. The night was going to be a long one. What would happen to her? The thought of losing her was making his knees weak. He needed her and Jacob. He realized how much he really needed them. Just seeing her lying there, pale and cold, nothin' he could do to help her. Nothin'.

Sam sat at Hannah's bedside while the hours passed. Star kept up with replacing bandages and reapplying the poultice mixture every few hours. He held her hand and only left her side a few times getting up to stretch and pace around in the room. Doc Turner later returned from the Lancets checking Hannah's progress. There was little to no change. He offered to stay with Star and Alvin, but they assured him he'd be sent for if there were any changes that needed him to be present.

"Alvin, one of us needs to go and check to see how the boys are managing with Jacob, I'll be fine with Sam if you don't mind. I just think one of us needs to be here to get him to rest. He's worried himself sick and I'm just as afraid for him as I am Hannah."

"Well, if your sure Star, I'll get back as soon as I can. Jacob is in good hands with the boys. But I need to see for myself how there handling everything. Go on and try to talk to Sam. He for sure is taking all this pretty hard."

Alvin returned to the Hannah's room, patting Sam on the back before leaving to go home. "I'm going to check on Jacob Sam. Is there anything I can do for you?"

"No Alvin. I'll be fine. You tell Jacob I'm still busy with his mama, tell him she's resting for now."

Alvin kissed Star goodbye and walked out of the quarters house, unsure of what he would be coming back to.

Star pleaded with him. "Sam, you need to get some rest. It's going to be a long night. She's going to need you when she pulls out of this so save your strength. The boys and Gennie will take good care of Jacob, I'll wake you up if there is any change. Now go on. There's fresh bread on the table and a few pieces of raw jerky for you to eat if you're hungry."

Sam walked out to the front porch and stood there for a moment.

He looked up to a clear night sky and a full moon. He could see the swing Alvin made for Jacob's birthday hanging from the tree in the brightness of the moonlight. That was a fine day. He remembered how happy Jacob was. Everyone was there celebrating his birthday. It seemed like that was a lifetime ago. He walked over to the swing and gave it a little push. He thought about how his life had changed since Jacob and Hannah came along. It sure wasn't what he expected. They were the thing he had been missing in life, and he hadn't realized that until now. He didn't want to think about how it might be if anything happened to Hannah. Sam looked up to the stars in the night sky and then bowed his head and closed his eyes.

"Now Lord, I just bet you never thought you'd hear a word from me. To tell you the truth I never thought I'd be havin' a word to give ya. I just want you to know how sorry I am that it took the chance of losing this woman for you to get my attention. You know if it hadn't been for her and the boy, I'd probably gone right on blamin' you for all the trouble in my life. I know now that it were'nt you that was to blame for Amelia. You had your own reasons, I guess. I'm at peace with that now. I can see that you had something planned a whole lot better than what I could have ever thought of. I've been bitter for a long time Lord. I was wrong, I'm sorry Lord. I know I don't have any right at all to ask you what I'm about to ask you. I tell you if you let Ms. Hannah get better, I'll be the best man I can be for you. I'll be at church every Sunday from now on and I'll close my eyes when I pray. I'll start readin' the Bible tonight and every night from now on. I'll try and live my life better. And you know me well enough Lord that I mean what I say. I promise I'll take care of her and little Jacob. Do ya think you could find it in your heart to see to it that she lives? I'll understand if you think you need her up in heaven. I won't like it but I won't t fuss about it either. After all you can take care of her a lot better than I can. I'll keep my promise to you about church and prayin' and the Bible no matter what way you decide. I got a lot to make up for Lord. Serita would sure be surprised after all these years of her houndin' me. Well Lord. Will ya study on it? I'll sure need your help to lookout for the boy if you take his mama.

Anyways, that's all I wanted to say. And Lord, thank you for sendin' Mrs. Martin. I sure appreciate it, Thanks for hearin' me out, Lord."

Sam walked back to the house to the room where Hannah was. He stood at her bedroom window looking out into the moonlight and he saw a shooting star. The room was quiet except for the crackling of the fire. He looked at Hannah's face for a long time before he could find the words, he wanted her to hear.

"Hannah, I want you to know I'm sure proud that the Lord saw fit to send you to me and the Triple S. I know it hasn't been easy for you. You didn't know you were gonna have to deal with a salty old cowboy. I hope I haven't tried your patience too thin. I tell ya, my life hasn't been the same since that day you kissed me on the way to Nightshade. I think about that a lot. I just want to say, you and Jacob are the best thing in my life. Now I don't know if you know it or not, I didn't want to admit it to myself, but I love you, Hannah. Did ya hear me, I love you. You just never forget that. And if the Lord sees fit to let you stay with us, I mean to ask you to marry me. So, you just hang on now, because Jacob and I need you. I'll take good care of you both, I guarantee it. I'll make a good husband to you and a father to little Jacob. The Lord has the last word on what happens to us. I trust him. You rest now. I'm not goin' anywhere. I'll be right here if you need anything,"

And with that he stood up and kissed her softly on her cheek. He saw her Bible laying on the nightstand so, he pulled the rocking chair beside her bed, opened the book to Genesis and read until he fell asleep. Star found him there holding Hannah's hand with one hand and the Bible with the other.

Alvin made it back within a few hours. Jacob was asleep when he left, balled up between Matt and Mark in their double bed. He had asked about his mama, and Alvin told him she was being cared for by Sam, but she was resting well.

"Sam sure looks worried Alvin. By tomorrow we should know if things are getting better. I'll leave him be. He fell asleep in the rocking chair, and I don't have the heart to make him move."

"He needs to be with her Star. And she needs him. Let's hope and pray that Doc Turner is right."

Star pulled a crochet blanket from the guest bed and covered Sam with it. It would be a long night, for them all.

# CHAPTER 60

The helpers' quarters was decorated with blue and yellow ribbons and bows. The afternoon was bright and clear. The chairs were arranged in rows side to side outside with people making their way to take a seat. Star and Naomi set the cake out on the kitchen table. There was a pitcher of cold water and lemonade available to anyone, after the ceremony. They worked most of the morning putting up ribbons on all the trees outside including the sycamore tree where the wood swing was still hanging. There were a few people in attendance from Nightshade, Grover the newspaper man, Mr. Barney, and the sisters, Ms. Sarah and Sally Frances. The whole Lowoods clan. Serita even came from Kansas to be there. A few folks from church showed up, those that were familiar with Hannah and Sam. The Reverend Mayweather and his wife were talking to Hannah and Sam on the porch. Serita was in conversation with Naomi and Star.

"It's a wonderful day isn't it Star? She's a lovely bride. I'm so happy for both of them."

"Yes Serita, I'd say it's happy all aways around. You couldn't have asked for a better day or place for those two to get hitched. We've waited a long time. I hardly slept a wink just thinking about it. Alvin too. Finally, after all these years the ghosts are gone, this house will have a regular family living in it again."

Naomi searched for Robert who was already finding his way to a seat up front. She excused herself from Serita and Star taking her place beside him.

Reverend Mayweather holding on to his Bible stood close to Hannah and Sam.

"Well, you look all fancied up there Sam, it's good to see you smiling on this happy occasion. I know you and Hannah are excited."

Sam tugged at his collar, causing his tie to be out of place, He fidgeted while Hannah fixed his tie, arranging it back to center. She turned to the Reverend. "It is a perfect day isn't it reverend?"

"I'm happy you agreed to do the marryin' reverend, it seems like it took long enough."

Hannah shushed him, "Oh Sam, you're a silly man. It took how long it was supposed to take."

"She looks especially pretty today Reverend. I got lucky don't you agree?'"

"Luck ain't the right word Sam, I'd say you both are blessed you found each other.'

Hannah touched her ring, spinning it around on her finger, nodding in agreement with the reverend.

Reverend Mayweather opened his Bible and faced the crowd. "Well let's get this thing started. I'm lookin' forward to eatin' some of Ms. Star's cake."

"Will the congregation stand for the sayin' of the vows?'

"Beloved we're gathered here to unite these two in holy matrimony. Now you two take each other's hands."

"Do you Jacob Joesph Martin take Genesis Ruth Lowoods for your lawful wedded wife?"

With a broad smile, a sparkle in his eyes and without hesitation he responded, "I do reverend, I surely do."

Printed in the United States
by Baker & Taylor Publisher Services

Printed in the United States
by Baker & Taylor Publisher Services